The cockroach knows
all the scurrying places
down on Insect Street.
More than that, it can
go to places no other
creature can go, into the
dark places, the slithering
places, the cracks and
crevices. The cockroach
can eat the darkness.
It eats away at the dark
walls nobody can see. Its
bronze shell protects it,
and enables it to make
the return to this visible
world. Thus it takes on
the ability to move from
one realm to another,
one world to another.

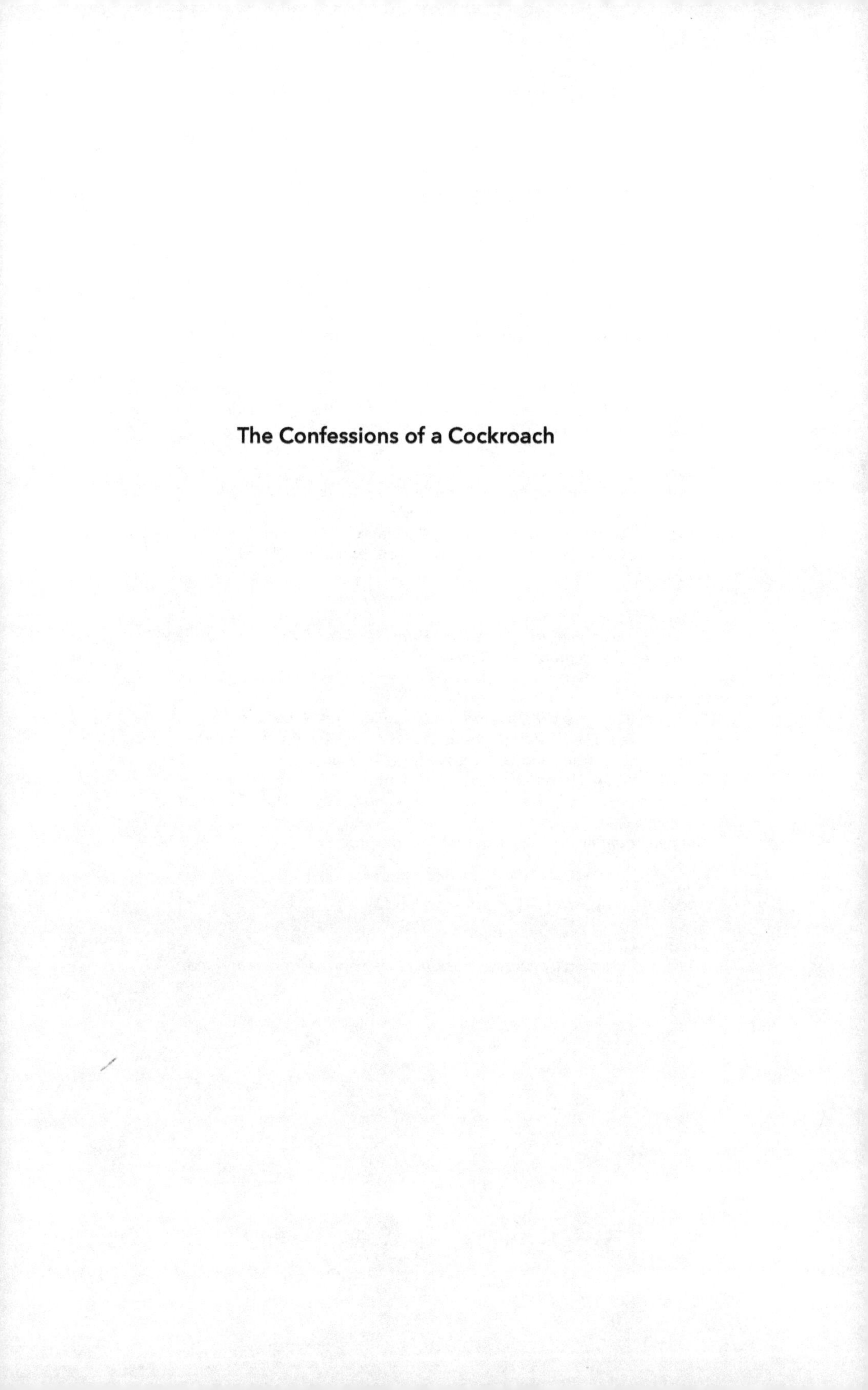

The Confessions of a Cockroach

Other books by Mike Johnson

Novels
Hold My Teeth While I Teach You To Dance, 99% Press, Auckland.
Travesty. Titus Books, Auckland.
Stench. Hazard Press, Christchurch.
Counterpart. Harper Collins, Sydney.
Dumb Show. Longacre Press, Dunedin.
Lethal Dose. Hard Echo Press, Auckland.
Antibody Positive. Hard Echo Press, Auckland.
Lear: The Shakespeare Company Plays Lear at Babylon. Hard Echo Press, Auckland.

Shorter Fiction
Back in the Day: Tales from NZ's Own Paradise Island. 99% Press, Auckland.
Foreigners. Penguin Books, Auckland.

Poetry
To Beatrice: Where We Crossed the Line. Pie Press, Auckland.
Vertical Harp: The Selected Poems of Li He. Titus Books, Auckland.
Treasure Hunt. Auckland University Press, Auckland.
Standing Wave. Hard Echo Press, Auckland.
From a Woman in Mt Eden Prison & Drawing Lessons. Hard Echo Press, Auckland.
The Palanquin Ropes. Voice Press, Wellington.

Non Fiction
Angel of Compassion. TP Press, Auckland.

Children's Fiction
Taniwha. Illustrated by Jennifer Rackham. Beansprout Press, Auckland.

'After finishing Mike Johnson's *Travesty,* and re-reading his previous novels and poetry, I have come to the conclusion that, with it, he has achieved the epitome or culmination of something. He has achieved a kind of "worldmaking" — to borrow American philosopher Nelson Goodman's famous term — that confirms his position as one of New Zealand's most important fiction writers.'
Judy Dalgleish, 'Half Way House of the Soul', Landfall.

'One of the most innovative, original and fearless writers I know.'
Witi Ihimaera

'Mike Johnson is the most underrated of all living New Zealand authors. Sometimes gothic, sometimes lyrical, sometimes both at once, his output over the past three decades has been extraordinary. Yet much of his fiction and most of his poetry has slipped by, barely reviewed.'
Iain Sharp on *The Vertical Harp: Selected Poems of Li He*, Sunday Star-Times.

'*Dumb Show* is a triumph... It's a rare item, a fully sustained poetic novel… Johnson is a writer who always tests the borders of fiction.'
Gerry Webb, Quote Unquote, 1997

'It's not often that we get a local novel of such verbal texture.'
David Dowling, Landfall, *Lear - the Shakespeare Company plays Lear at Babylon*

The Confessions of

a Cockroach

Mike Johnson

99% Press

Published by 99% Press,
an imprint of Lasavia Publishing Ltd.
Auckland, New Zealand
www.lasaviapublishing.com

ISBN: 978-0-473-39766-1

1

The moment I sit down... I become... invisible.

Invisibility becomes me.

Now you see me, now you don't.

The moment you see me, I slither out of sight.

Let's say there's more to this vanishing act than meets the eye.

As long as you don't make any sudden moves in my direction, we can keep it this way. We don't have to put it to the test. Instead, we can put it all to rest. Nobody will blame us. In our position, they would do the same.

I would invite you to sit with me, pull up a piece of pavement and make yourself at home, but I don't want to implicate you. People can be quick to draw conclusions and slow to change their minds.

I don't have to struggle to become invisible. I don't have to put up a fight. I don't have to bear the burden of any action. Exercise any special powers, or utter any incantation. I don't have to execute any enemies. It just happens. There is no exchange of fluids. All I have to do is let nature take its course, let gravity guide me to the ground. About half way down.... I vanish from sight.

You might think I had vanished down a man-hole.

My first feeling is that of relief, followed fast by a touch of dread. Dread and relief flow through me like clear and muddy streams that intermingle. Dread, because I know that this is my final and irrevocable condition, and relief because I don't have to look up any more, or pretend to be anything more than I am. Or am not. Although, sometimes I do look up and take a quick peek at the world. Like a child playing hide-and-seek... I must cover my eyes and count to a hundred. Sometimes I do. But when I open them nothing has changed. Only the light has moved on. No one hides, except the girl with the skipping rope. We should talk about her at some stage, because the rules don't apply to her.

Sitting down is a significant moment in the life of an invisible, even if it doesn't take any effort. Even if no one notices it.

Upright, and at eye height, I am fair game. Like a car on a railway crossing. Or a rich man in a dark alley on a hungry night. There is nowhere to go. No avoiding it, whatever it is. Upright and walking I'm a target. A target for hit men and bill collectors and angry officials. A target for eyes with no other target.

On my bum, on the street, eyes collide without me, or the dubious benefit of my intervention. No longer do I come between people and the things they want to look at. No longer do I smudge the view. I sink out of sight the way a dead fish might sink into the water, quietly and fast fading. Invisibility follows quickly after. Being invisible is like sitting on the bottom of the ocean. A little light filters in from above. Creatures of all shapes and sizes glide in and out of vision. The world undulates gently within its perceptible wavelength.

The world in a hubcap.

But none of that matters. I have found somewhere to sit. A place to occupy. I have my little piece of invisibility. My stake in the un-world. At least until I am moved on. No matter how invisible you are, you can always be moved on. Invisibility offers no immunity in that regard. I mean from the forces of law and order. Invisibility doesn't cut any ice with the boys in blue; they have heard it all.

2

So you are back again. I wasn't expecting that. I wasn't expecting anything. For me that is the key. Sometimes a coin falls out of the sky, sometimes it doesn't. I can't count on it. Sometimes a person will walk by, sometimes they will stop. Sometimes they will shout abuse, sometimes they will blow kisses to the air. Sometimes they will carry their heads under their arms. At night you may hear gunfire; at dawn you might hear the call to prayer. En-masse, there is no accounting for people.

After I sit down, none of that matters.

15

The moment I sit down, invisibility envelops me.

How I achieve invisibility is quite simple. As I have explained, it takes no special abilities, no athletic prowess. Anyone can do it, that's the beauty of it. Even a fool. Even a wise man. My legs fold under me like a folding chair. I collapse through space like a dead star. A moment later the hard pavement collects me; the rough wall at my back reminds me. Now I am no longer seen. Now I am in everybody's blind spot.

Welcome to my world.

Light waves fail to penetrate this cone of invisibility. They bend around it. See! There is nothing here. Just bent light. The rest is mere imagining.

It is like the caul in which some babies are born. There is a fluidity in it. It doesn't welcome me, it doesn't reject me - it is indifferent to me. It is another medium, a medium people move through but never see. People move through invisibility as if it doesn't exist. They push it aside with the wave of a hand. They pierce it with their laser eyes. They don't see that it is threaded through all things the way silk might be threaded through cotton. The way dark matter is threaded through light. They don't threaten to fall into it with every step they take. They trust the visible world as a blind person trusts the tap of a stick on the concrete pavement. Here I might lend my weight, they think. The weight of their bodies. The weight of their pasts. The weight of their walking. The way people walk, they are leaning into the future. For them the future is something visible, like a horizon line in the dawn. Like a marmalade morning. A walk in the park.

It's not like that for me. That is what you wanted to hear, is it not? You must be here for a reason. Everybody has a reason. Everybody has a horizon. There's a walk in the park just down the road from you.

The invisible line without the benefit of horizons. I am home again, where it all started. Back inside my caul. Although, it is not really home. It's just a familiar place, with familiar smells. A place where I can play the ghost and get away with it. For all practical purposes, I am a ghost.

You can count me out when it comes to physical sports.

3

I have my favourite spot. It is at the bottom of a set of once quite grandiose steps that lead up to what was once a rather grandiose bank. It's all ornate stone and empire. The steps lie in a semi-circle between two Greek pillars that stretch up to cornices and balconies far above. It was designed that way, I believe, to induce a sense of awe in those passing up the steps and between the pillars into the hushed house of money. Since money is not very awe inspiring in itself, just mostly dirty bits of paper, it needs a bombastic setting in order to instill the proper reverence for the money god.

The door to which the steps lead is now closed for good. The god has moved on, downsized. Gone virtual.

In this case an old door made of oak with thick bands of steel reinforcing and painted dark green. Respectability and rectitude. And very shut. With a little imagination, it might be the door to a castle, or prison. You could imagine it clanking open with a solid sound. If you knocked on it, it would feel like hitting armour.

Now of course the bank's interior has long gone. The steps lead nowhere but to that door which never opens. Only the façade remains. Behind that façade lie all kinds of shops and even a tattoo parlour, accessed from a mall just down the street a bit. Kings Mall, it's called, for no good reason.

Above the columns, attached to the stonework by an iron hinge, is the large round face of a bronze clock. Like a double-edged sword, it faces up and down the street. Towards the past and towards the future. The hours are marked with Roman numerals and its hands are tipped, like arrows aimed at the heart of the hour. It is a clock heavy with history, redolent with empire, the clock face as ornate as the filigree ironwork that holds it in place.

The men who made this clock must have believed in fate or destiny. That there was something momentous in the movement of time in those days, in the clanking forward of the arrow from one marked minute to the next. It carries with it the weight of everything.

For me there is no fate and certainly no destiny. A coin will either turn up on my enamel plate or not. Sometimes there are coins, sometimes there are none. There is no rhyme or reason for this. It just happens, as I've already tried to tell you. If there is a fate, it has passed me by long ago. If there is a destiny, I have already beggared it. I am immune, which is some compensation for invisibility. If I am quiet enough and still enough and humble enough even the gods won't notice me, I figure.

Sometimes money just comes to me, falls naturally into my hands or my enamel bowl without any interventions. On one occasion an interesting set of legs approached. A confident man, but, and this is rare, a man of intuition. He was swinging his arms. In one hand he bore a coin, doubtless change from a recent transaction that he hadn't got around to putting back in his pocket. So it floated there, between his fingers, like a ripe fruit about to fall, and as he passed me, all I had to do was lift my hand to meet his, which was descending, and the coin slipped from his hand into mine with no conscious volition on his part. In fact he was surprised to see that it had gone.

No clanking armour of destiny there.

This clock stopped a long time ago, perhaps when the dark green door closed forever. It stopped at twenty to eleven. People like to joke that a stopped clock is right twice a day, but for how long, I ask? Time is not a piece of string. It doesn't measure anything. Time is the master of moving on. Move on, please, move on, and it does. Until it can move on no longer.

Time moved on for this clock a long time ago. Its minutes and hours have been consigned to history. Twenty to eleven is a random moment the clock's failing mechanism has captured for a hundred years or more. That particular twenty to eleven has been lost forever. Sometimes I imagine what was happening at that twenty to eleven. A bank clerk was pulling at his sleeve. A buggy was pulling up at the door. A gull was flying overhead, looking for the ocean. A poor man sat down on the steps and never rose again.

A stopped clock is a piece of history. It has given up. Given up trying to keep up.

Giving up time or the world is not the same as forgiving the world. Or time. Many of my fellow invisibles suffer from a muffled resentment, a choked up rage. Overwhelmingly, they did not choose invisibility, but had invisibility thrust upon them, like others with their greatness. When their twenty to eleven arrived, they were not ready. Nobody is. The invisible must resent and envy the visible, for the visible are usually well fed.

Perhaps you want to know if I resent and envy you. That depends, but one thing I know, I wouldn't want to be you. To carry all that worry, to court all that fear. I suspect you are one of those people who are always looking for meanings. But what is the meaning of a star, or a tree, or a hair on your head? Or twenty to eleven?

In the absence of meaning, you look around for fate. Or destiny.

And if by some marvellous chance the arrows on the bronze clock moved on to nineteen minutes to eleven, what would that mean? Would anyone even notice? Except me? You see, the clock too has become invisible. It became invisible at twenty to eleven.

4

I often see people coming and going from the tattoo parlour, some of them proudly bearing their new tats. Or others with virgin skin, eager for the needle. Even on a cooler day, the newly tattooed will wear singlets to show off their illustrated shoulders, or shorts to show their patterned legs. Tats are all the rage nowadays. You see them everywhere, on all kinds of people. It is easy for me to understand why people love getting tats - it makes them more visible. How proud and happy they are, bearing their designs to the world, knowing they will be looked at by avid eyes. They will be seen. And it is in being seen that they exist. They feel real in the avidity of others. They have not embraced their invisibility - far from it. In fact they have devised all kinds of stratagems to avoid it.

Not a single one of them would envy me, or dream of changing places with me. To them, to be invisible would be a living death.

How much easier it is to look at people's legs rather than their faces. Their legs tell me all I want to know, but don't look back at me. Except once. Some fool had tattooed eyes on his knees.

I have become a connoisseur of legs. Yes... I know you will laugh at me for this, or think me perverted or rude, but it is merely an aspect of my condition. If you sit on the street at leg level, you become a connoisseur of legs whether you want to or not. You become an expert in footwear.

To lift my eyes above the level of a pedestrian's waist is to compromise my invisibility. It disturbs people to meet the eye of an invisible person because, for just that moment, the invisible becomes visible, and a tremor runs through us both. A tremor of recognition. So I have become a connoisseur of legs. And footwear. Their age, their stage, their state of mind: the legs and the shoes show it all.

Some like to show their legs, as far as their legs will show. And further. Some like to demonstrate that legs end in the swell of the buttocks. Some like to swaddle them, or veil them, or outline them in tight fabric. Some are shy, some are blatant. One man always wears a long dark coat, no matter how warm. It isn't just his legs he wants to conceal. Yet his pulled-up socks always ensure that no piece of flesh shows anywhere, even on the hottest day. Maybe he has iron legs. Or a skin condition. Or his shame runs so deep his flesh shies away from the light.

I know all kinds of things just from the lower half of the human body.

I know immediately who is rich, who is poor, and who is just pretending. I know who is conceited, who is humble and who is out to kill or love. I know who is sick and who jogs for ten kilometres a day. The invisible know the visible, but that doesn't work the other way around.

I know who is lost and who is a thief, who is insecure and who win-wins, who is innocent and who hasn't paid, who is compassionate and who carries a knife, who dreams of death and who dreams of sex, who loves themselves and who loves the world, who's found the world and who's lost it.

I learn many intimate details. With women I can tell who is having their period, who is pregnant, who is ovulating, and who had sex the night before. With men I can tell who's had a vasectomy, who's got an erection, and who's had sex the night before. It's all in the legs, the feet and the footwear, and the way they move through the air. It is not hard to do this, again you don't need any special abilities or enhanced perceptions - all you need is to be invisible for long enough and much will become visible to you. The legs are a dead giveaway.

If two people are walking together, I can tell if they are a couple, friends, acquaintances, or just happen by accident to be walking side by side.

I can even tell, from the subtle change in an approaching set of legs, if the person is going to give me any money or not.

If you sat down with me, by my side, you would see. It doesn't take too long to get the knack of it. But I can see you are too scared.

Look at all these legs going by now, as we have our little chat. Look! Some are like spring rain, some are like the moon. Some are like thunderbolts, some are like stray dogs, some are like dripping candles. Some are alive and some are the walking dead.

I tell you it's a knack. You'd pick it up in no time.

My own legs I keep mostly tucked up underneath me, safely out of sight. I have learned that it doesn't help to have them sticking out in front of me in an unsightly way. If I put my begging bowl where my legs should be I attract more coins.

And that's the art of it. To be a grey smudge behind my enamel plate.

5

You have to understand that giving money to invisible people is a problematic thing for anybody.

Your money drops through a hole into nowhere. Your money becomes invisible as it enters invisible land. It may sit in my plate all day, boasting to the world, enticing others, but to you it has become invisible. It some odd way you're having a hard time figuring, your coin has lost its meaning, its value even. It has become a shiny thing in a plate. You have no idea what it will become, a pie, pint or proposition.

You're not buying anything, not even gratitude. In fact, you are just throwing money away.

One day I was approached by an excitable gentleman who told me that the day before he had thrown a fifty-cent piece into my plate and made a wish. And the wish had come true. How amazing! He thought he had been throwing his money away, but actually he'd been buying favours from Wishland. The hole through which his money dropped led to the world of the fairies, the wish-granting type. My humble enamel plate was not a begging-bowl but a wishing-well.

Certainly I wished him well.

All of a sudden his spent fifty-cents had a meaning, a pur-

24

pose.

I remembered his fifty-cents, and suggested that he double his money. If fifty cents could buy the granting of a wish, what might five dollars buy? A ticket to Paradise? He wouldn't stretch as far as five dollars, he didn't want to get too ambitious, he said, or disappointed if nothing came of it, but he stretched as far as a two-dollar coin. Half way to Paradise. I didn't see him again, so I guess it didn't work out. My wishing-well must have lost its luster. Or, he'd wished himself right out of his life to be some other person somewhere else.

It comes down to acknowledgement. Your coin is not a pledge; it is an admission, no matter small. Small is okay. Beggars can't be choosers, right? Your coin is just a throwaway, but it lands in my tin.

To acknowledge an invisible, is to accept, in some insidious, passive way the existence of the whole invisible world which, for a disturbing moment, seems to rise up around us and take material form. Dark walls. Marble skies. The groan of the oppressed. To acknowledge invisibility is to momentarily at least transform the world. Disquiet rules.

Then there is the question of how other passers-by might react. When others witness somebody dropping money into my enamel bowl, and they hear the eternal sound of coins striking metal, they too have to see the invisible world thus revealed. Most turn their heads away and prefer not to see acts of charity, as if there were something shameful in them. When they turn their heads away, they don't see the dark walls. They

don't feel the sun clanging off the marble sky. They don't hear
the past crying out loud. Their own lives have slipped over the
horizon.

6

Being invisible has its advantages. Being known and seen by
the world is not all it's cracked up to be. I see plenty of people
in the great passing parade who would trade places with me in
a flash if they understood my relief and could deal with being
ignored.

Not you, of course. You understand me too well to envy me.
I wouldn't try it on you. You at least have paused for a moment
in your busy life to think about it.

Much of the fear and revulsion with which people react to
us, even to the skipping girl, is because we are everybody's mirror. The mirror of their fear. *There but for the grace of god go
I,* they think as they hurry past, as if destitution was nothing
more than the withholding of god's favour and nothing to do
with economic realities. *There but for the grace of god...*

I can see that pity is a great comfort to people. You are allowed to feel pity for those who have fallen out of favour with
god. Or the financial system. Much the same thing from my
perspective. You may fall on hard times the way you slip on an
icy patch of pavement. It's too easy to despise pity. Pity is like
a swamp. It sucks everything under. But I don't mind it. Like
greed, sometimes it works.

26

An attractive lady with elegant legs brought me a falafel out of pity. She ordered it and waited at the takeaway as it was being made. Then she brought it over to me. Pity made her body shake. I saw her hesitation in the turning of her knees. Her voice was low and kind. Perhaps I reminded her of a relative, someone she felt guilty about. She knew people would be watching her giving a falafel to an invisible person. They would see her ignoring the sign that says 'Do Not Feed The Cockroaches'.

She was very well dressed. I'm sure everybody normally looked at her approvingly. She wore five hundred dollar shoes, by my estimation. All I know is that they were dark red and polished to a shine. I could see my own shadow in them as I accepted the falafel.

It was a big one. It had everything in it.

I think it was you who said that the universe itself is a mirror. We are everything people fear and dread because, at a twitch of fate or the money markets, they could be us. They – the rich and the visible. The visibly rich. The get rich quick and the get rich slow. It's always just hanging by a thread, and when the thread snaps... you find yourself sitting on the pavement with me, staring at people's legs. Accepting a falafel from a lady with fancy shoes and a moment to spare.

You have told me that it is fear and greed that motivates the human world, at least the financial side of it - love gets squeezed in the middle there somewhere - and when fear rules, people dream of invisibility with a fierce dread and anticipation. Fear and greed make us visible. Like a target is visible. To be visible is to be a target. That's why I say that being invisible has its advantages. Fear and greed mirror each other, and it's hard to stay visible in the human world caught in between.

I see many fearful legs. And footwear. The way they move, the tension in their passing, the twist of a knee or the tight outline of a calf muscle. Often that tension increases as the legs approach. That is because the invisible is a mirror of the visible. We are them, and this is what frightens them. They fear what they can no longer disguise. What they can no longer despise. They see themselves slipping into the invisible world the way a drowning man slips beneath the water - that's how they would describe it. How they perceive their lives. One turn of the screw and they are down here with us on the street with our begging bowls and our pitiful eyes.

As I say, there are advantages to being invisible, which is perhaps why some people hate us. Hate does strange things to a person's walk. Just as love will loosen a person's movements, hate will tighten them. Hate will turn leg muscles into knots. A person who hates looks as if he or she is trying to move in two directions at once.

Invisibility is no protection from hate. It attracts it. Sometimes people stare in my direction as if I were getting away with something. It's amazing the way the rich can think that the poor are ripping them off. They look at me suspiciously as if my invisibility was lifestyle choice adopted at their expense. Perhaps they see a cockroach and resent that it can slip between the cracks.

Hate dries everything up. Nothing moist can survive, especially tears. This drought mainly affects the hater, leaving that person desiccated and twisted, but at the same time a hateful person likes to spread it around, give people the evil eye at every opportunity. Hate is the ultimate form of judgment. It is a citadel. It is a way of keeping out the world. Love is a way of letting the world in. You let the world in when you drop a penny into my plate. You let more of the world in if you drop a couple of bucks.

Cruelty is the natural expression of hatred. Without cruelty, hatred has nowhere to go. Once a person came by wearing brightly coloured trainers and track pants and scooped a nice fat coin out of my enamel bowl. And laughed. Stealing from a beggar is a hell of a joke. It was not the taking of the money that was to do the hurt, but the laugh. It was not a petty laugh, or the laugh of a fool who thinks he has just made a great joke, but a laugh full of broken glass. A way of telling me that the only good invisible person is a dead one. Death is the ultimate invisibility. The desired outcome. That laugh was an invitation for me to die, right there and then. It was a door that opened to a very cold place. The laugh was to tell me that I was not welcome in this world, that I have no place here, in the interstices of the streets where the invisible seem to breed. The laugh was to tell me that I would be better off dead. That death was preferable to being a worm. A worm that any passing foot might squash without compunction. It was a laugh that had no compunction.

My comfort was the knowledge, gained from many hours of contemplating shoes, that the trainers were fakes. Their owner had been duped, or wished to deceive the world. In a world full of fake appearances, this did not surprise me.

I saw those brightly coloured trainers again, a few days later, passing by me quite slowly. I didn't look up. I knew this person only wanted to steal from me again. In this case, however, there were no big fat coins to be taken. Just small thin ones, beneath his contempt. No fun in taking small coins.

A few days later the game took another turn. A second set of trainers turned up, as fine and brightly coloured and fake as the first, attached to some manly, hairy legs. This person dropped a note into my enamel bowl. Not a large note but a significant one. Enough for several days' food. I left it there, as an inspiration to others. It looked very fine and dandy sitting there, slightly curled, in my chipped and humble enamel bowl. Slumming it, perhaps, but fine and dandy nevertheless. I took some time to admire it, and the rugged visage of one our national heroes on one side.

A moment later, as I am sure you have foreseen, the second set of trainers came along and the note was whisked out of my bowl. This time there were two sets of cruel laughter, each mirroring the other. It seems that cruelty likes company. Now my bowl had only a few pitiful coins in it. I vowed that the next time they tried that trick, I would snatch the note as soon as it hit my enamel bowl. They didn't return. Perhaps they knew that their trick would not work twice.

7

Part of being invisible is having no past. Twenty to eleven is not a past. Only people of substance have pasts. A past is something good money can buy. You can carry a past in a handbag with your compact and your pepper spray. You can have a bottom drawer full of it. You can hire storage units to store it. A past is something you can measure in things. *Penny-wise, pound-foolish.*

Sing a song of sixpence sang the nursery rhyme. Nursery rhymes have bonnets, don't you know.

I have nothing to boast of. Nothing to write home about, they say. And nothing to write it with. So, memory can find no foothold. I have an invisible past, which is almost as good as having no past at all. I know it's there, for I can feel its breath. I can feel the tug of it on my mind, like the tug of gravity. Sometimes there's enough of the world in place for me to have the sensation of falling. The past is all there is to break that fall, but that never happens, at least not to me. It takes a while for the past to dissolve into invisibility to the point where it no longer exists. It takes practice. Practice and fortitude.

Sometimes I think the girl with the skipping rope is from the past. My past, your past. I have no evidence for this. It is just a feeling, a tug on my mind. A lightness in her step, perhaps. Or a particular old-worldly sound to the song she sings under her breath whenever she skips.

Lost my partner, What'll I do?
Lost my partner, What'll I do?
Lost my partner, What'll I do?
Skip to my Lou, my darlin'.

... a pause while she does a few skips and takes a few breaths...

Skip, skip, skip to my Lou,
Skip, skip, skip to my Lou,
Skip, skip, skip to my Lou,
Skip to my Lou, my darlin'

While this is her favourite rhyme it is not her only one. Occasionally, someone will ask her to skip. She has a regular. A woman in a brown coat and old-fashioned stockings with seams. She always looks as if she has lost something. She will take out a crumpled five dollar note, smooth it out in her hand so the girl can see it, and say - Skip them all! Skip them all!

And the little girl will. She will show all her skips. As she does so, she sings out loud:

The High Skip
The Sly Skip
The Skip like a Feather
The Long Skip
The Strong Skip
And the Skip All Together!
The Slow Skip
The Toe Skip

The Skip Double-Double
The Fast Skip
The Last Skip
And the Skip Against Trouble!

The Skip Double-Double is particularly impressive as she can jump just once to a double swing of the rope. *Tippity-tippity tap.* Sometimes people clap when she does that. When she does the Fast Skip the rope disappears in a whirl of motion and so do her feet. When she does the High Skip she can skip right over the moon. I've seen stars glimmer on her footwear, which is light and soft, like ballet shoes.

When she Skips like a Feather, she seems to have no weight at all and will float to ground just like a real feather with a side-to-side movement.

This will make the woman in the brown coat smile. A smile on the face of someone who has almost forgotten how to smile is a wondrous thing. Now she looks as if she has found something. She moves on, carrying the smile like a trophy.

There is another world here, on the plane of invisibility. The world of invisible things. The girl with the skipping rope is one. I believe she can skip from world to world with that rope, but contents herself with a strip of pavement, where it extends into the road to serve the bus-stop right by. I have watched people - they will step around her but do not see her. She is like me. And because she is like me, she can see me and I can see her. We can see each other. But what's the point? It doesn't change anything about the world.

The girl with the skipping rope can see me, but most of the time she pretends not to. She is more like a busker. People give her money for skipping, because she can skip so fast the rope turns into a blur and her feet hardly touch the ground. The faster she goes the more coins fall into her cup. Sometimes I get the feeling that she could skip right up to the stars if she wanted to, if she didn't want to alarm people. She is not a cockroach. She is a hummingbird.

Sometimes I catch her smiling. Invisible people are not supposed to smile for it makes us too visible in the wrong way. How can a smile be a secret? The skipping girl's smile is secret because no one wants to give alms to a person who might be happier than themselves. A sad, grim or crestfallen expression is best, so no one gets offended.

Others do things to try to make themselves more visible. Like the living statue. By not moving at all, not even blinking, but holding some particular pose, he often has people standing around watching him, throwing a little money into his cup. I think they are waiting for him to move, to make a mistake and reveal some sign of his humanity, then they would be freed from the obligation to give him money. But he's too good for that. He can stay frozen for hours if needs be, apparently freed even from the need to breathe.

He doesn't blink, not even when a coin falls into his cup.

8

Being invisible means being voiceless. I may sing, but no sound emerges. I may cry, but only in another world. I may shout, but only to the empty air. That doesn't apply to you of course - you always have a ready ear. And there are others, mostly invisibles, who sometimes speak to me out of their invisibility. Jinee is one of those. She never makes much sense, but she hasn't forgotten how to talk. 'Have you got any ciggies,' she'll say even when she knows I haven't. It used to be that people would throw down still smoldering butts for an invisible like Jinee to seize, but hardly anyone smokes in the street anymore or throws their butts on the pavement. The rubbish bins are a better bet for her but that doesn't stop her from keeping a vigilant eye on the pavement.

Compared to Jinee, you are my perfect listener. There's nothing you don't hear, and perhaps, I can only conjecture, nothing you don't understand, which is a comfort to me when the wind blows cold, but Jinee doesn't listen. When I talk to her, my words turn into confetti. Confetti tossed into the air on her wedding day, which may be the only day in her life she remembers with any clarity - unless she made it up. All she thinks about now are ciggies. She even calls herself Ciggy Stardust. She always has a little hoard stashed about her person, and she is always patting her body to make sure it is still there.

She is not the only one who can hear me. Sometimes a man comes up and says things to me. He is not invisible. He is a

Christian and he is on a pilgrimage to the City of Gold. He has a duty, he told me, to bring the invisible into the sight of god, because before god no one is invisible. But god himself is invisible, I said. God is one of us. He didn't like that but felt it was uncharitable to feel that way.

He was very uncharitable when I told him that I was really a cockroach. If I could wear a badge or patch it would be a cockroach. The cockroach knows all the scurrying places down on Insect Street. More than that, it can go to places no other creature can go, into the dark places, the slithering places, the cracks and crevices. The cockroach can eat the darkness. It eats away at the dark walls nobody can see. Its bronze shell protects it, and enables it to make the return to this visible world. Thus it takes on the ability to move from one realm to another, one world to another. The humble and despised cockroach is the harbinger of the supernatural. These people walking past, who would happily stomp on a cockroach, don't know that. They have no idea. If they stopped and sat down with me, they might begin to understand.

The Christian is a very nice man doing his best. Doing his duty. Shaping up before god. He has a very visible smile. Being nice is a point of honour for him. He always brings me something to eat. He tells me that I should identify myself with something more uplifting, and is disturbed by the notion that the cockroach has a supernatural aspect. To him these are no more than errant thoughts, bred out of long hours of boredom. He suggests that I turn my thoughts to more noble and ennobling things, like the life of the saints and the shining example of the saviour. He would happily banish the cockroach to the dark worlds forever. For him, the blood of the lamb is poetry, the squishy insides of the cockroach is not. Each to their own, I say, but that does not appeal to him.

I don't mind talking to him though, while I am aware that for him I am only partially visible. In that respect he is like Jinee. He sees fragments of me, and tries to assemble me out of those fragments. I have to be patient with him. He's only doing what he has been trained to do. I have to learn to live with my partial visibility where he is concerned. I have to avoid trying to show him things he can't see. It's as if he can see my toes but not my foot, my knee but not my thigh, my bowl but not the hands that hold it. I can understand that. My hands are not so pretty. They are the same dusty colour as the pavement, the same colour as my clothes. My camouflage. He may look at my toe and see a cockroach, look at my knee and see a carbuncle, look at my cup and see poverty – but he doesn't see me. I am hidden amongst all those other things. I can't blame him for that.

Before I learned that it was better to stay silent and chastened when he was about – the idea that poverty itself is a penance is as deeply ingrained as it is dreary – I told him about some of my memories. How I remember taking a buggy ride to a hardware store. The road was very dusty. The shop was full of axes and saws and pickaxes and spades and shovels and sledge hammers – all manner of instruments for cutting and tear-ing and ripping and digging. Men were standing around with long beards and fixed stares while women in bonnets scurried about like pet rats. The Christian man told me I couldn't possibly remember such things. I would have to be at least a hundred years old to have a memory like that. It would have to be a made-up memory. Apparently we all have them. They are created out of things we have read and heard. I reminded him that I was a cockroach, and could therefore go places others could not go, into the invisible places, and return to tell the tale.

He doesn't understand that. But then, he is not a cockroach. He is a jackal, but I can't tell him that. I'm sure he would have a negative opinion of jackals. He's not the kind of person to take a broader, more ecological view of scavengers, and how important they are for taking care of the more messy messes of life, rotting carcasses and the like. Smelly things. After the beasts of prey come the jackals. Like the cockroach, the jackal is a creature of the dark. Of furtive places. Their job is to pick the bones left by the predators, but, on occasion, they hunt in packs, like dogs. The invisibles are a little like those rotting carcasses. It's handy to think of nice Christian people running around tidying up messes, like me, doing a little spiritual cleansing, trying to make us visible to the angels. Scrubbing down the steps where we sleep. Then perhaps we will, like their saviour, miraculously arise and pick up our shiny things and join the walkers and no longer take up space on the pavement.

I have to humour the Christian man. Play along. Be his fall

guy. Pretend that we really are equal in the eyes of god and the law. I do this by nodding and touching his arm. Not because I can't speak... you know that I can... but that I have learned it is better to hold your peace, and be humble in the eyes of whatever god is holding the purse strings. Buddhists are a bother because they don't have a god and tend not to carry cash. It can be nice, however to feel their universal compassion washing over me as they go past. It is instructive to be, even momentarily, in the company of an Awakened One.

Once I stopped humouring him and asked him, seriously, why his god sometimes snatched coins out of mid-air, before they could reach my bowl. He was confused about that, and I'm afraid I became a little excited. Once I knew it all, I told him. Once I lived the ages of man. I gave Socrates his poison, kissed Jesus on the cheek, sent the moon down out of the sky to harass Mahomet. I married a princess. I wove gold from straw. I waited on dogs that sat at tables and barked at people. I recited all the names of god until the stars began to disappear. Now all I do is sit here and bow my head. All I do is wait. With a bowed head. Wait without hope, because I have abandoned hope. I have lost any claim I had on hope - now I fall back on charity. I wait for a penny to hit the bowl. I can wait for days. I can see the wolves gathering at the end of the street; their patience is wearing thin. Is it fair that god should snatch my coins out of mid-air? They leave the willing hand of the giver, but they never get to hit the bowl. I don't hear the sounds of charity ringing in my ears. Is god in such need?

The Christian man was quite taken aback by this irrational outburst. I felt quite shame-faced. After all, how many times have I told myself, and probably you, that we have no business expecting things to be fair. Fairness is not built into the situation. The street slopes. Some struggle up and some cruise down. And I can't do anything about the wolves. They will go on gathering until their time comes. Some coins will hit the tin, some will not. Every coin is equal in the eyes of god.

I know that the Christian man is not alone. Sometimes I see another, like him, hovering at a distance, watching out for him, watching his back as the saying goes. A member of the pack. That man is a jackal too. I think one day he will move in on Jinee. They both want to pick me clean so that I am naked before God, tear away the last sinewy bits of the world, the ligaments and gristle, so that I am nothing more than polished bone.

Mostly he contents himself by bringing me filled rolls, but once he brought me a fish pie. It smelled like the ocean and tasted like heaven. He told me that if I let his god into my heart, I could eat fish pies every day.

I am beginning to wonder if the Christian man is becoming invisible but doesn't know it. Slipping into our world without noticing. Just up the street from me there is an older bearded man with a banjo and his pitiful wife. She plays a battered old mandolin. I don't know where they sleep or what they say to one another in the morning. They are invisible too. He sings and sings songs about Jesus and the blood of the lamb as if he wants to be heard. Their voices float on the wind, but nobody hears them. People hurry past, taking no notice of them. This couple makes the Christian uneasy, for they are Christian too. If they can end up on the street, with a battered banjo case open before them, he could go the same way - except he can't play any musical instrument.

I like the singing couple better than the Christian man. They never waver. Even in the cold, the old man's fingers can find the notes, his voice can find the words. They are staunch, that couple. Their pride never falters, even when the wind blows at its coldest or the heat suffocates them. They have much more faith than the Christian man who talks to me. He talks a lot about faith but his voice is full of doubt. Perhaps the reason he gives me alms is not because of his faith but because of his doubt. He would give me cheeseburgers to keep his doubt at bay. I'm not complaining.

Once he was sitting with me, and had put his beanie down beside him to wipe the heat off his face, and somebody threw a coin into it. That gave him a shock. He looked at me with wide-eyes. For a moment he experienced what is was like to be invisible. I didn't see him again for some days after that.

9

My begging bowl is more like a plate than a bowl, although quite deep, one of those enamel bowls manufactured for camping. It is without pretentions, unless you count the blue strip around the rim. Not every enamel bowl can boast a blue rim! Its undistinguished off-white surface would have come up quite shiny clean at one time. It still does, in places. Mostly it is very finely scratched from the movement of coins on its surface.

There is quite a large chip out of one section, leaving the dark metal showing. For all its battered humility, it is my most precious possession. My only possession. It is the sort of item you might buy at a garage sale for twenty-cents and end up regretting the purchase.

Some might think it a little bold. Some use their beanies. I don't like that. A beanie looks too squishy, lying on the pavement. Almost dissolute. Besides, when the wind blows cold I like my beanie on my head.

Since it is my only possession, I am very careful with my enamel bowl, battered and chipped as it is. You could call it my lifeline. The bowl has been around, but like me its history has been obliterated. I found it in a rubbish bin, where Jinee searches for ciggy butts. Too old and damaged to be of any use, I suppose. It fitted my purpose quite admirably, although some might think it a little showy.

I have studied this bowl at great lengths, being a natural thing to look at while I am sitting there on my bank steps, and I can assure you that it has no hidden meaning, or beauty, or anything else. It reveals nothing about the world, but merely what it is. It doesn't aspire to anything. It offers no fascinations.

In the hierarchy of dinner sets with their hard-fired patterns, the enamel bowl is an invisible. The very lowest caste. It wears its humility without any visible signs of envy. It has no desire to become a Royal Doulton. No maker ever desired to put a stamp on the bottom of that bowl!

Across the road there is an invisible we call the rat man because he has a pet rat or two secreted about his person. And so he should. After all, who is going to want to give money to a man crawling with rats? He has a nice, dark, polished wooden bowl. It looks like a leftover from a life he has lost. At night his rats like to curl up and sleep in it. He can see all sorts of things in the grain of the wood, all sorts of things revealed by long hours with nothing else to look at which stays still. There's a whole geography there. Hills and cosmolined landscapes. Knots of suns and stars. When he studies his bowl, he sees the whole universe reflected back at him, all the lines of energy and gravitation. Even the echo of creation. It's all there, in his polished wooden bowl.

To drop a coin into such a bowl must be like dropping a stone into a very still pool.

Nothing like that is possible for me and my enamel bowl. There are no energy lines or echoes there. No hints of a good life now gone. No hints of fallen circumstances. Just an impervious enamel surface. Impervious to the eye, that is, not the world. The world may continue to chip away at it, make inroads into it, create ugly spots of rust where there was once a smooth reflective surface. Otherwise it is a territory without maps.

When you drop a coin into my bowl there are no ripples, just a dull, hard, commercial sound.

Yet, hardly worth a second glance, it tells me all kinds of things. With my eyes closed, I can tell if a dropped coin is of gold or silver by the sound it makes on the enamel. If the tin feels a little greasy it is going to be a humid day. If it shines as bright as a button there will be good luck. If I can see my face in it, then I am growing weak with hunger.

Because hunger is what it's all about.

My bowl is a signal of my status and role in life. It announces me. It marks me for what I am. It is the visible token of my invisibility. People may see it, and put money in it, without seeing me. While it announces and marks me, I can also hide behind it. You need look no further, sir, madam, scumbag. What you see is a begging bowl and that's all you know and all you need to know. And a beggarly bowl it is!

I am the smudge in the air behind the bowl.

And I am mostly hungry.

Sometimes, as the skipping girl skips, I chant under my breath,

Lady, Lady, drop your purse
Life is sweet but it could be worse!

Such things have happened. You wouldn't believe the stories!

Here's one for you, for your little book of anecdotes. I heard of a woman who tossed her wedding ring into a beggar's cup without even pausing in her step. Or it might have been a man. One way or another, the marriage was over. The ring turned out to be worth more than a thousand dollars.

One day, two miracles happened one after the other, separated by only a few moments as clocks tell the time. Somebody put a full, unopened packet of cigarettes into Jinee's hat. It was a deluxe pack with twenty-five death-sticks inside, all white and shiny. Jinee snatched it up almost before it hit the ground, in case it never hit the ground. She could barely contain herself, barely control her hands as she tore at the cellophane wrapping. She feared some cruel hoax, a packet full of grass clippings or dog excrement.

Before she could get it open, however, the next miracle occurred. Someone dropped a hundred dollar note into my enamel plate. I didn't snatch it out of the air, I watched it as it as it slid and rocked gently down, seemingly taking forever. Jinee and myself were mesmerized by the sight. I have seen some leaves fall like that, rocking like little boats at sea.

Neither of us quite knew what it was we were looking at. It featured a famous scientist, and a ghostly watermark of the Queen of England. It felt right and smelt right. It was a genuine banknote, just as Jinee's gift was a genuine packet of death sticks. Oh, weren't we the queen and king, if just for a moment. We were the envy of every invisible on the street. Jinee sat back and triumphantly lit up, blowing the smoke into the air with huge satisfaction. She looked as if all her Christmases had come at once. Soon some of her friends, like PC would come along to share in her good fortune until it was all gone.

I slipped the hundred note into one of my inner pockets. A note like that can make you visible to predators. The street is full of stoats and weasels and all sorts of creatures with sharp eyes. They usually take no notice of the invisibles, but not in a case like this. I hundred note might as well glow in the dark.

I know that one day I will find a use for it, and that day may come sooner rather than later. That is the rule of thumb here in the land of the invisibles - if you can imagine it, it may already be happening.

Destitution is not in itself invisibility, but goes with the territory. The rich have a hard time effacing themselves from the world. For them, wealth is like people's tats, it makes them visible. Those thousand dollar suits and five hundred dollar shoes have one purpose only - to be seen. By the right people of course, but also to make the wearer an object of interest, like a landmark or famous building. What use would they be if everybody was blind? Even if you owned the Mona Lisa, it would be meaningless if nobody could see it. It would have no more meaning than an empty canvas. If you burned it, you would not see the colours burning brightly in the flames.

10

Sometimes I am convinced that the city consists of just this one street, that it extends only as far as I can see, which is just up the road a bit. That doesn't make any sense, I know. Here there are four directions, just like everywhere else, and a sunny side of a street, with lots of passing feet, that might go on forever. Pull out a compass and it would have no unsettled premonitions.

All these walkers and vehicles and cycles passing across my frame of reference, my little patch of street, must come from somewhere and be going somewhere. Those people on busses, the street must keep on unfolding in front of them. Around another corner and another street unfolds, complete with buildings and bus stops and slices of sky. I think of it like a magic trick the universe plays. If I take a few steps one way, the universe will take a few steps backwards, conjuring another few steps of world. Just for my benefit, it seems. If I were to peek around the shop front and up that alley along the road, buildings and shop signs and sandwich boards would obligingly present themselves. In this game of cosmic peek-a-boo, you can never catch the world absent, even for a moment. Not this side of the speed of light.

I know how ridiculous I sound. I can see the smile on your face. After all, if this little piece of street is all that exists, where does everybody else live? Take everybody's piece of street and put them all together and you have a world. Look out into space and you have a cosmos. If you want to know where somewhere is, your GPS will tell you. They don't call it a global positioning system for nothing. There are coordinates and you can be located using them. And me.

A quick, surgical laser strike from the sky would prove the point.

And yet... and yet, friend... it doesn't feel like that to me. This one piece of street on which I live, such a life as it is, is like an ice floe. It bobs about in the cross currents of the visible and the invisible. The world breaks off at the end of the street. There will be other ice floes, bobbing about, grinding up against one another. At night I can hear that grinding sound. One day I might have to seek them out. When I get moved on.

It is a perfectly ordinary piece of street. It slopes steadily and gently from the bay to a ridge that partially circles the bay. Naturally enough, foot traffic moves faster downhill than up. I get more money from people moving uphill. Perhaps in that fractionally longer time it takes for them to pass me, the possibility that someone might find a loose coin they can part with increases. Or perhaps people feel a shade more compassion when they have to push against gravity to keep moving. We remind them what will happen if they stop moving.

Above the veranda line, you can see something of the city's history, what's left of it. Lots of stonework. Lots of stern effort to be memorable. There is a woman sitting across the street in a nice, deep shop doorway, no longer used. She is my mirror. When she looks across the street, which she does quite often, it is me that she sees. She never waves or shows any sign of recognition, which is how it should be. Invisible people should be invisible to one another, even if they are not. Visible people, good citizens and bad, become disturbed if the invisible begin to band together and show too much coordinated behaviour. To be properly invisible you have to be separated from others.

Whether the woman across the road appreciates any of this is beside the point. Perhaps she is half blind and can't see me. None of that matters. She is still my mirror and I am hers. When I want to know what I look like when I hold up my hand for alms, all I have to do is watch her doing the same thing. Such an abject gesture, and yet it requires no rehearsing. No rehashing. No polishing. It comes out perfect every time. And it is as ancient as begging itself.

Alms! Alms!

Sometimes, when the light is right, it rings off the gold or silver coins people throw into her hat. I can see the flash even if I am looking the other way. I'm sure she gets more coins than I do. Once I saw a note fluttering into her hat like a sad moth that had lost the dark.

11

Jinee has a friend who doesn't smoke. We call her PC, which is short for Pipe Cleaner, because, in order to have something to do with her restless hands, she makes pipe-cleaner animals and imaginary creatures which she pretends to sell to children. She doesn't really sell them because children never have any money. She prefers to give them away. Sometimes people give her cigarettes. These she hands straight over to Jinee. I think this is the real basis of the relationship, because Jinee has no interest in pipe cleaner creatures, except to take them apart from time to time to see how they are made. Or stick dirty, used ciggie filters onto the legs to make nicotine stained shoes. This annoys PC, because Jinee can't put them back together again. PC has to straighten them out and start all over.

PC only turns up from time to time, which makes me think she is a part-time invisible. I suspect she does have a place to go to, but prefers being on the street. I think it pays for her to go invisible from time to time. Her face is ravaged by self-pity. Her arms and legs are often covered by bruises inflicted by somebody with no pity at all. She drags herself along as if her body is unwilling to be in the world. It is clear to me that she must be subject to some terrible abuse she cannot speak about.

I have to say, she is not the only one. There are many among us who have arrived here via abuse of one form or another. You can hear it in the voices we use to talk to ourselves. *Stupid girl!* PC will say when she gets one of her pipe-cleaner figures wrong. *Ugly Muggly! The only thing you are good for is for the dog to piss in your mouth! Open your mouth, Ugly Muggly, and let the dog piss in your mouth!* She mutters stuff like this as she fashions her little furry wire creatures, trying to reconstruct her psyche as she goes, and not getting very far.

I think these part-time invisibles have a harder time of it than anybody. They are neither one thing nor the other. They are too mad to be either here or there. They are inbetweeners. On one hand, they fear invisibility and cling to the trappings of the world as hard as they can; on the other hand they take refuge in invisibility when the world grows too many fists. Only on the endlessly busy street can they find true anonymity. At last, a place where nobody will recognize them because nobody can see them.

Oddly, the police began to harass PC while completely ignoring me and the skipping girl. If you are invisible enough, not even the police can see you - unless they look really hard. PC, being a part-time invisible, doesn't have that immunity. The police seemed to be concerned about her pipe-cleaner creatures. It seems that some of them had sharp pointy ears that might be used as a weapon. A child might jab another child in the eye with a pipe-cleaner rabbit, they said. This in fact had already happened and a parent complained. They are only acting on a complaint, they said. They wouldn't have bothered otherwise. They wouldn't have asked her if she had a permit to sell pipe-cleaner creatures on the street. One of the cops was a woman with a nice blonde ponytail that bobbed about every time she moved her head. It was a very self-righteous little pony tail, I must say, for she was clear in her opinion that PC should move on, should stop making lethal little critters, and take her sorry self home. Where, perhaps, she could get the care she deserved. Perhaps. It all became a little vague at that point.

PC, I must say, was quite clever in handling this situation. Without fuss or argument she packed her pipe cleaners away. Only very slowly. She has a pencil case she uses for this purpose, and one by one each pipe clear was carefully laid inside. It took her ages. The cop with the ponytail got impatient.

Boy Blue was around at the time, and he came out of hiding to help her, which was very brave of him given his abject fear of authority. He took a giraffe that had a very dangerous looking neck and began to play with it, galloping it up and down the steps to the old bank, with not a single indication of wanting to poke somebody's eye out with it.

A couple of days later PC returned with some fresh bruises and carried on with what she was doing.

Boy Blue was pleased to see her. He scampered about like a silly puppy, up and down the steps.

Boy Blue was really too little to be invisible. Usually invisibility does not become a possibility until puberty or after; little kids tend to get noticed. Little kids need mummies and daddies to look after them. Little kids on their own tend to cause distress in people, whereas I cause hardly any distress at all. We called him Boy Blue because he never told us his name. Perhaps he couldn't remember or had never had one. His skin had a slightly blue tinge, as if he were cold all the time, even in the stinking heat.

One day Jinee and I were sitting on steps of the old bank watching the passing parade, every now and again lifting up our hands in ritual supplication, when a little boy with blue hair slipped in between us and tried to hide amongst our beggars' rags. He desperately wanted to become invisible. We looked around to see if anyone was in pursuit, an anxious or wrathful mother or father, for example. A concerned aunty. But nobody came running. It seemed that the whole world and everything in it made him afraid. Jinee thought he had strayed from an institution, because that's what she did, or came down in the last shower, which is what people sometimes said she did, or that he grew in a field of flowers and was raised by roses, which is what she would like to have happened.

The first thing she did was ask him if he had any ciggies.

I could see that he was another cockroach, like me, and that he had strayed through some crack in the world to this place and now he couldn't find his way back again. This might happen from time to time to cockroaches. I thought that eventually he would find that crack in the world and return to his own street. I think that about myself, sometimes, that I will find a worm hole or a rabbit hole or just a plain old manhole and return to some place where I am no longer invisible and the light pours out of the sky in shining rivers of gold. Perhaps I'll see the Christian there.

Boy Blue stayed around, and for a while his grubby little hands got more coins than mine. That happened more often when Jinee was there and it took me a while to figure it out. People were giving him money because the three of us looked like a down-and-out family. Father, mother and bedraggled child. When I figured that out I decided to keep quiet about it, but Jinee had got there first, and felt she had the right to take a share for herself, most of it in fact, and did a vanishing act of her own. The absconding mother. She doubtless used the money to buy cigarettes, the only shiny things she has ever cared about. And she wouldn't come back until she had finished smoking them, in case we guessed the truth and tried to take them off her.

So for a while there, on the steps of what was once a bank, unwittingly we played our familial roles without doing anything different. Just having Boy Blue around did the trick.

I think sometimes he scared the money out of the punters' pockets.

12

Did I tell you about the one who came among us called Pablo? That's what he called himself. The bewildered one. He was one of the lost, and a very long way from home. How it happened he couldn't quite explain. It all happened too fast. Or he was too slow. He was a tourist, he said, a backpacker, but his backpack had been stolen. That was the beginning of his slide. He turned around one day and found himself without any money or friends or even a useful language on the main street of a city he hardly knew, with his cap in hand. Later, he got me to write on a piece of cardboard the following message to all the people. *Please help me. I have been robbed and stranded here. I need to buy my ticket home.* This he conveyed to me with signs and signals and extraordinary facial contortions.

I believed him. Some of the invisibles write such signs, which they can hide behind, but in most cases they are lies.

They just want to make it through to the next day, or buy a drink.

Pablo didn't embrace his invisibility. He had to be dragged kicking and screaming into it. It was not a pleasant sight. When he became aware of what was happening to him, he became very frightened and agitated. It was incomprehensible that his life should end here, in this way, fading from sight on a strange city street. It was like dying. It was worse than dying.

Funny thing is, we found out that Pablo had money. Quite a lot, in fact. Two rolls, one for each shoe. That's how I found out. I could see by the way he minced along that he had something there, so I asked him outright. Jinee thought it was very funny. Her face screwed up like a squashed mango. Pablo was very paranoid about us finding out, and extra paranoid about Jinee laughing at him. If she thought he was so funny, she might share her joke with others. He tried to explain, using lots of foreign words and hand shapes, that he still did not have enough to get him home, the only place he wanted to go. Home was somewhere, here was nowhere. He only had enough to catch a plane to some other nowhere, and there was no advantage in that.

But what about a room and a bed and a soft pillow, I asked him. I wish now I hadn't asked that. It put him into an agony. He could do that, he could get a room for the night, he could feel, if only for one night, that he was no longer invisible, that he had rejoined the human race. He could sit at the backpackers' café and have a cup of coffee, with cream, and nobody would be any the wiser. Nobody would know. But even as he did this he would know that he was slipping backwards, further from his goal, as his coffee turned into coffee and a croissant, as his rolls of money grew thinner, a fact he would be reminded of with every step he took.

He was able to convey this so vividly that I assumed it had already happened to him, perhaps more than once, his sense of hopelessness increasing each time as the realization took hold that he was never going to get back home. Not ever. Not unless a miracle happened.

Well, why didn't he buy a phone with the money and ring somebody. Get some money sent. That suggestion provoked an even greater outpouring of words and frantic hand signals. After all, this was modern day and age, with GPS and mobiles and all kind of apps. I didn't ever figure out what the problem was, but apparently he couldn't do that. I began to wonder if he was a criminal of some kind.

Pablo found it very difficult to stay still, let alone sit with the kind of dull quietude invisibility requires. Sometimes he would jump to his feet and do a little scuffling dance, attracting the disapproval of passers-by. Or he would ask the skipping girl for a loan of her rope, which she would steadfastly ignore. Or he would begin talking to somebody in his language, which might be Portuguese but which might be something else, some dialect variant. Perhaps he could only speak Basque, or some obscure language. He dreamed that one day he would talk to somebody and he would talk back and he would be saved. An angel would descend from the sky and lift him up, up - and away.

That didn't happen. I'm not quite sure what did. Perhaps the boys in blue got him. The boys in blue get very interested when the invisible make themselves visible, in other words, make a nuisance of themselves. Invisibility then becomes vagrancy, and the prospect of ending up in some institution in which invisibility is both impossible and yet mandatory. These are only suppositions. The invisible world is a transitory one. People come and go like ghosts without explanations. That's because the invisible have lost their history like Pablo, or never had one, so there is nothing to explain when they disappear. Pablo became terrified when he felt his history slipping away from him. He might've rushed off in pursuit of it. There are those who think they can chase after their identities the way a child chases after a butterfly. As if the past can be trapped within the mesh of mind. Since it is doomed to fail, this hopeless pursuit can have bitter consequences.

Perhaps there are levels or planes of invisibility through which one can slip. Jinee and the skipping girl and me are kind of stuck on this particular plane of invisibility, which operates more like a social stigma than anything else. And yet, it may be possible to slip further into the invisible world and meld with empty air, abandon the fiction of the body for once and for all. In this case Pablo might still be around, in another dimension, feeling even more abandoned.

I know that you might be happy to entertain that possibility, since you are the perfect listener, but the Christian man didn't like it much. He said I was trying to comfort myself with silly fancies, and that it is more likely that someone found out about the rolls of money in his shoes and beat him up and robbed him and left him for dead. I felt sad when the Christian man said that, perhaps because it might be true. On the other hand, he could only say that because he was not invisible. He could leave it there without feeling the shadow of the dark walls. He is happy in the dream of his god, and always leaves me with a satisfied look on his face. The look of a man who has willingly done his duty.

13

Being invisible does not make me impervious. I am not invisible to the wind, or the cold, or the stinking heat, or the fumes, or curious dogs. In fact being invisible leaves me exposed to the elements. If I were visible, I would not be so unprotected. I could pop into a café to cool off or warm up. It seems unjust that the cold should notice me while people do not. Not only does the cold notice me, it seems to seek me out. It slides along the pavement in active search of victims.

I am not impervious to the hard concrete under my backside, the grit of fumes in my eyes, the rough sounds of the city in my ears, the hunger of the street. The world rubs up against me, rubs bits off me, pounds me to a single consistency, a single hunger, a homogeneous discomfort.

If you are waiting for me to make a fine speech about how my invisibility is a blessed state, more blessed than being rich, you will be waiting a long time. A piece of rotting garbage may be more blessed than me, for at least it has a natural and assigned state.

We are the human waste discarded by a culture built upon waste, and we have no natural or assigned state. No papers, no pensions. And no way out of pain but desperate and makeshift stratagems. I am not giving up the world when I sit down, I am giving in. Caving in. Going belly-up. My invisibility is a confession of defeat - I'm sure that's the way you see it. Those who lose their jobs speak jokingly of being tossed on the garbage heap. You can hear them from time to time, bursting into nervous laughter as they walk past. Hello! from the garbage heap.

It's tough at the bottom. Below the bottom, that's Insect Street.

Already these punters can feel invisibility eating into their flesh and it's not a pleasant feeling. The voracious air is kissing them with mouths full of needles. They can smell the garbage heap. They look around fearfully to make sure people can still see them. They pat other people's dogs to make sure the world still exists, that they still exist. They check their bank accounts to make sure that flesh-eating bacteria has not evolved into some money gobbling glyph. They do up their buttons to keep themselves in. They are terribly afraid of any leakage. Any slow, unnoticed ebbing away. One morning they may wake up, search for the sun and not find it, walk down familiar hallways and not find their door, pass through the streets voiceless and unseen. They are afraid of turning into ghosts before they have even died.

In other words, they are afraid of joining me. Afraid of that moment of terrible transparency when they admit defeat and slump onto a hard bench or in a stinking shop doorway. In that moment the whole world can see them.

I have no comfort to offer them. No reassurance. They don't give me money for that. They give me money to keep me at bay, not to invite me into their lives. The elegant lady who once bought me a falafel would never invite me into her home, because by coming into her home I would make her homeless in some psychological way. I would make her feel homeless.

You might be tempted to think that I am a bit of dreamer, making the best out of a bad job, as it were, making up compensations, finding silver linings where there are really only dark clouds. I believe you are mistaken. I am not about to tell you that I am happier than that rich man with the Italian shoes I see twice a day, once in the morning on his way to his money factory, and once in the evening when he is returning to his very visible home and his very visible spouse in a street doing its best to be bright and shiny.

Bright and shiny is not on the menu for the invisible.

The hard concrete doesn't grow softer with time. I may only be half in the world, but it is the half that hurts.

You have sometimes described the house the Italian shoes

man lives in somewhat contemptuously as a McMansion. But why should you, even the most perfect listener, assume that I share your values and your attitudes? Put me in a McMansion and I will not complain. I would be happy to live inside a Christmas cake. I could eat my way out from the inside. I would be in cockroach heaven.

14

I'm happy for you to talk to me, and play the perfect listener, but I wouldn't want you to get the wrong idea. About me, I mean... I wouldn't want you to think that you are talking to some settled identity. A real identity has a set of certainties and parameters you can recognize, a status and personality. Not me. Like a kid's colouring-in, I slop over the designated outlines. I spill this way and that. This makes it a bit messy for everybody.

Every now and again someone will come along and try to clean up the mess and attempt to assign some stable markers to me. Someone like you. That's when the trouble begins. What is your name? What is your father's name? What is your mother's name? What was your last address? When were you born? That's when the trouble begins, always started off by lots of questions.

To be invisible is to lose specificity, eventually. I am nothing. Just a smudge across space and time. A blur sitting on the steps of the old bank, in between the falafel fast food joint and the merino wool tourist trap. This is my last address. I was born here. My father's name is National Bank. My mother is the skipping girl. I was married once to a woman who gave me a falafel.

You see, to have a real and proper identity you need a real and proper past and a set of memories tried tested and true. You need bag and baggage. You need a clock that isn't perpetually trapped at twenty to eleven. You need all kinds of things that I don't have.

That's why you're finding it hard to get an exact fix on me. However you triangulate me, I'm not quite there, not quite that. I slip out from under. Do you really think anybody would want to pay me for that, even though it is quite a trick and involves all sorts of subtle forces? It's not like being able to make pipe-cleaner animals or skip over the sky.

Nothing is to be expected of me, and in return I can expect no outcomes from the world. Even from you. Ultimately you have the choice, the power. You can come and go as you please. You can talk to me or walk right by. You can put a coin in my bowl or keep it in your pocket. At least in the meantime you can do these things. You can boast a certain coherence, I'm sure. You know where your skin ends and the world begins. You can feel the world rubbing up against you. You have vowed to give it a fair go. You like your life, and why shouldn't you. After all, you're not often hungry. Your legs work fine. You can walk through streets that are continuous and connected. You have a top drawer full of bravery awards and condoms. You are no stranger to hot water showers and morning coffees.

You are the outcome of all those choices you have made over your life.

I have choices too. Do I sit on the bottom step or the second to bottom step? Do I turn my plate around so that the chipped bit faces outwards? Do I turn my head up the street or down? Do I put out my hand, palm up, or do I just sit here? Do I say my piece or hold my peace?

I can choose to starve, if you call that a choice.

I have these choices but no power. No power over people or things. To be powerless is to be choiceless. I can't come and go as I please, not if I want to keep my spot on the steps. The only power I have is to ignore the world and be ignored by it. To be in the world but not of it. To be among beings but not of them. To talk to you and not be heard. To make no claims and seek none.

To be a smear in a world of droplets.

Invisibility is not a choice. It is a medium. It is a condition. It is a contradiction. It is a final insistence upon dignity where there is no dignity. Invisibility was not something I ever chose, as if I could have somehow weighed up the two worlds like two options, and made a rational choice. That is a mockery, of course. In the land of fear and greed there are no rational choices anyway. Rather, invisibility stole up on me like a thief in the night. A cloak of unbecoming, it slipped over me when I wasn't watching. Like the man in the story who woke up one morning and found he'd turned into a beetle, I woke up one morning and found I was sleeping on cardboard on the side of the street huddled under a grey blanket that wasn't mine. A piece of human thistledown, I found I had no substance. The wind blew right through me. My cage of bones dissolved in dawn down the stone canyons, these same stone canyons.

Mostly, except for you, the world communicates to me through one simple mode - the fall of a coin into my enamel plate. As if the world and I share only one word, and even then the world is niggardly with its use. With one short syllable, the coin hits the plate. Or a quick double syllable. Clink-clunk. I am that enamel plate. No more than that. Its blue rim is my circumference. Right there is my identity. I may only get one or two words a day from the world, and these words may be poor coin. Not every day will I get a hundred dollar note, or any kind of note, for that matter.

To be invisible is to be forgotten. People cannot live without their forgetfulness. Too much remembering would weigh us down intolerably, I appreciate that. I like to forget too. I forget yesterday as quickly as today. We need to forget in order to move on. There is a pleasure in forgetting. I like to forget each day as it occurs. Why should I accumulate the days? I am not trying to prove anything. I am not keeping a diary. I am just as happy for the past to slip behind me as the next man, but there is a particular kind of forgetfulness that rules the passing parade. They may see us, but must forget us in the very instant of their seeing. Or the instant after. By the time they have moved on a step or two, they have forgotten they have ever seen me. It is as if they have never seen me. It's as good as having never seen me. My invisibility resides in the forgetfulness of others.

I slip through the paradox.

They talk of sweeping unwelcome things under the rug. Well, here we are, under the rug. Not even peeking out.

Out of sight out of mind.

15

If I want to, I can see the world through the wide-angled lens of a shiny hubcap. That one you see over there. Every day the same car is parked there for the morning in front of the bus stop, where the skipping girl skips. I see the owner quite regularly. He has scuffed shoes and the creases are long gone from his trousers, but he always keeps his car's hubcaps bright and shiny. I imagine him cleaning and polishing them. Every hour or so he will appear from somewhere and feed the parking meter.

His hubcaps give me a unique view of the world. People passing by suddenly look very bulbous. They loom in the wide-angle of bent light. A world hammered back at the edges, rimmed in light.

They serve to remind me that things are not always the way they look. The hubcap is like an eye that reflects what it sees. I can see with that eye if I want to. Sometimes I can't help myself, for that eye is full of moving shapes and, when the sun is right, slices of light.

The fact that I might see the world through the intermediary of the hubcap reminds me of the uneasy paradox of my position. Being invisible doesn't necessarily mean that people don't see me. It's just that, in most cases, they see me but look away before that seeing can register. To be invisible means to be seen and not seen. As in a hubcap - a shape, a bar of stretched light.

I don't have to be seen exactly in order for people to put a coin into my enamel bowl. They may see the bowl but not me. Or they see me, but it is only a quick furtive look, hardly offered before it is withdrawn. People are superstitious about meeting the eyes of the invisible. Acknowledgment suggests complicity. Complicity breeds guilt. My enamel bowl is like the hubcap. It offers people a view of themselves. Their bulbous pockets. It offers people a view of me, the cockroach attending the plate, a bit of dirt on the step.

For my part, I have to show myself, display my invisibility. You can hide inside your poverty from everything but hunger. Hunger rules. Invisibility becomes more obvious. Forgetfulness costs more. You may put a penny in my plate. And another.

Charity is a penance. An atonement for the sin of wealth. Although the wealthy will tell you wealth is no sin, they don't really believe it. The Christian man told me that god wants everybody to be prosperous and as full of abundance as nature itself. So how can wealth be a sin when god has urged us all to go forth and prosper and multiply like the fruit on the vine. Or fruit flies. Everybody wants to live a guilt free life. I have seen those wealthy ones who boast a guilt free life. They have a particular walk which bespeaks a strong sense of entitlement, and a determination to show the world what a guilt free life is like. So they make themselves visible by buying big shiny things, and small glittery things, and walking along like kings and queens.

They look at themselves in the hubcap as they go by and are gratified by what they see. It's a big, shiny world and it should reflect them. It should show them swaggering past. Looming up in sudden self-importance and dwindling fast as they move on.

I am not sure about all this, I have to confess to the nice Christian man who only wants to save my soul. He hasn't seen the look in the eyes of people who give me money, or the people who don't. Or even in your eye. That furtive, guilty look of those who glance at me and say to themselves, there but for the grace of god go I. And since, therefore, god has given them all this money to keep them from a graceless state, god must favour them over others, less fortunate, like me. So they deserve their money. Every penny of it. Every shiny hubcap of it.

The term penny pincher is not just figurative. I have seen it happening. People squeezing and pinching the coins in their pocket as they pass me, as if trying to imprint the pattern on their very fingertips.

In the early afternoon the man with the scuffed shoes drives the hubcaps away. He never sees me. He can walk around me and not see me at the same time. This is quite a trick, and he has perfected it.

For him, there is no paradox of seeing me but not seeing me, of acknowledging my invisibility in order to disavow it. For him, my invisibility works to perfection. He doesn't see me, he doesn't see the skipping girl, he doesn't see anything - only the parking meter, the car and the hubcaps.

Perhaps he catches a glimpse of me in his hubcaps, a glimpse that catches him unawares. For a moment, the real world.

Me sitting here.

Me in my cockroach kingdom.

16

While the Christian man sometimes brings me food - he likes beef sandwiches - I tend to rely upon my regulars, those few for whom dropping a coin my way has become a habit, something they don't even think about. It's easier for them not to think about it. You aren't in that category. You bring me things and you do think about it.

What use your thoughts are is another matter, but at least you struggle to keep me visible, and I appreciate that. My regulars don't worry about that sort of thing. A coin or two does for them, and does for me. I know where to find pastries when the bakeries are closing. I can get a whole bag for a dollar.

For my regulars, their coins are a substitute for thought. But they are still good people, every one... I wouldn't want you to think that I despise the people who give me money. It's not like that at all. But, you have to understand, nor am I that grateful - depending of course on how hungry I am. You have to be careful with gratitude. It can frighten people away.

I have a man who wears very sharp merino trousers with reinforced socks. A left-foot sock and a right-foot sock, properly shaped. I know the kind, very expensive. He comes by twice a day and always has a coin ready. He gives to the skipping girl too, and seems to take a moments pleasure when she stops skipping and gives him a quick courtesy. She does it so sweetly, just like a real little queen. It's an Alice in Wonderland act.

I have another regular, a woman with sensible shoes and strong, practical legs. I can imagine her as the mainstay of some family. A solid workhorse. The sort of person everybody takes for granted and won't be appreciated until she's gone. Whereas Merino Trousers tends to drop his coins from a height, enjoying the clang of coin on tin, Sensible Shoes bends right down and almost places the coin in the bowl. As she does this, she turns her head away, as if there is something of interest on the other side of the street, and all I see is a curtain of brown hair streaked with a little grey. I can imagine this woman feeding a stray kitten with warm milk.

My most unexpected regular is a teenager, a girl with soft moccasin like shoes that look a little like ballet shoes. White ankle socks are just visible above the shoes. She began by stopping to admire the skipping girl, but gave me a coin instead. I think she envies us, just a little, especially the skipping girl. There is nothing she would like better than to skip all day, skip classes, skip friends and peer pressure, skip the bullies, skip homework, skip right out from under, in fact. Perhaps giving us money is like making a promise to herself that one day she will be free of all these things, the huge demands of the world. She mistakes our invisibility for freedom, but I can forgive her for that. With every coin she drops into my bowl I forgive her more.

Not so many regulars when you think about it, although you have to count the Christian man. Just enough maybe to keep me here, on these same steps, and not move on, find some sheltered doorway, like the woman across the street.

Sit here long enough and all the world will pass by. Only a few will ever be back again. The commuters, they put their heads down and dash for their trains or their busses. Sometimes I think of going somewhere but it becomes harder and harder to imagine any place that would be so very different from this. In the end one piece of street is the same as another. If I moved up the road a bit, it would look different at first but soon it would be the same. The same old same old, people say. The street would resettle itself to accommodate me.

The passing parade and regular or two.

You ask me if I ever see things that are not there.

That's a strange question to ask. How could I see something if it's not there?

Perhaps you think that being invisible means I can see invisible things. Perhaps you sense that there is more to the street than meets the sky. Perhaps you see me as some kind of keeper of secrets. A guardian to the door of another world. That's fanciful. You've caught a vision of a street full of holes, that's all. And I've crawled out of one of them. And now you think I have some kind of second sight. That's rich!

What can a cockroach find in the dusty corners of the street? And why should you care, or even want to know what I can see or not see.

I don't quite know what you're getting at, whether you are concerned about my diet or the state of my mental health, but you have to understand I live in the same world as you. I suffer under the same sun, seek shelter from the same rain and run from the same wind. True, at night I will disappear through the cracks of the world, deeper into insect street to find a shadow to shelter me - but even you could follow me if you would, or if you were a cockroach. If you could squeeze yourself down to my size. If I see things that you don't see, that is not because I am seeing things that aren't there. You have to be very careful with your logic when it comes to these matters. Double negatives pile up like infinity signs.

Take the skipping girl, for example. You see a girl, skipping on the pavement, growing tired in the heat. But I see a being who might pass through worlds or skip through galaxies. See how she closes her eyes when she is skipping hard. She doesn't have to see the world anymore. She closes her eyes and the world, unseen, whirls around her until there is no world, no hard pavement beneath her feet. She is skipping through the cosmos. The whirling rope is her cosmos. The stars swing hectically in their orbits. She is a star, pulsing every millisecond. Sometimes people just stand and watch her, fascinated. So fascinated they forget to put a coin into her cup. They don't understand that the sound of it, their generosity, will ring through all time and space.

So what am I seeing? Only the invisible can see an invisible. I did see one who was in the wrong world. He was a beetle, not a humble cockroach like me but a royal scarab beetle, fresh from rolling the sun across the sky. He had that odour of sanctity about him. Somehow, in the twilight, he arrived on our street and walked up it, probably seeking a vantage point, confused and frightened. That sort of thing can happen because the whole multitudinous universe is full of holes, not just the street, not just your mind. I knew as soon as I saw him that he was from another world, that he'd slipped through a crack in space, and was starting to wonder which god he should blame. I called out to him but that frightened him even more. He much preferred not to be seen, and I don't blame him. Like everybody else, he passed out of sight. I never found out what happened to him.

But what would you have seen? Someone dressed in foreign clothes looking like they didn't quite know where they were? Not an uncommon sight in a city full of tourists. Perhaps you wouldn't have looked at him twice. You wouldn't have seen that he was well on the way to invisibility, which may, I suspect, ultimately turn out to be his route home. I doubt that you would have seen a scarab beetle, or a sungod, caught out after curfew looking for his home beneath the horizon.

I saw a vampire once too, scuttling up the street. He was a sad, pathetic creature and nothing like the romantic evil portrayed in books and movies. He tried to hide his face because hunger was written all over it. His thin, frail body was twisted by it. His eyes were red with it. His face was creased with a bat's mouth. He saw me but he didn't stop. He didn't like the look of me. He wasn't used to being seen for what he is. He did pause to sniff at the skipping girl who was putting away her rope for the day, but didn't linger. He knew my eyes were on him. Either that or the girl had the wrong smell.

So I have to ask you, do you see things that are not there? You see me, don't you? You incline your head in my direction when you speak. You are, after all, my perfect listener.

The question is not, what do I see. The question is, what can't you see? It's not that I can see things that are not there, it's that people deny things that are there. It's a game they play with the real world. If I don't like it, it's not there. That's a helluva way to live, my friend.

If you deny me, I don't go away. In fact I grow stronger. If you deny the world, the same thing will happen. Those who deny me give me power. This they can never understand. Their thinking is very superstitious, like the child who believes that if he squeezes his eyes tight enough shut the world won't be able to see him. All he needs to do to hide is shut his eyes. When I shut my eyes, the world goes away, he thinks. I see a storm coming from the west, but when I look to the east, the sky is bright and clear. Why then should I not look to the east all the time? When people say there is a storm coming, I can say with all honesty that all I can see is blue sky. And that wind tugging at my sleeve is just the wind. Nothing more. There has been wind since the world began. Why should I care? That person sitting on the street is invisible; they always have been. The poor will always be with you. Get over it. Drop a coin into the cup and forget about it. Where you come from, there will always be more coins, more poor. Forget about the storm, forget about the rapping at the door, forget about the crying of children, life can be lived in a great forgetfulness and sealed with a forgetful death. You can look the other way while death steals up on you, you are welcome, you thief in the night, because I can't see you. I can't see you because I have my eyes screwed shut.

To deny so furiously is to court hallucinations. The child who screws his eyes so tightly shut begins to see things, plays of light and shadow on the inside of his eyelids that threaten to turn into creatures, worlds even. At that moment it becomes much safer to open your eyes. To deny the world is to invent an imaginary one. You can do that, but living in that imaginary world is another matter. It takes a lot of energy, a lot of will. It is exhausting. And even the imagined world never quite turns out the way you hope. There is always a stone in the shoe. The telephone rings and the world is at the door. Birds sing and the dogs go to war.

If you were ever to become invisible, these things would be visible to you, but that is not why you are here. You have quite a different agenda of which I know nothing, but sometimes, I have to confess, I wonder if you have a life. If you have life, what are you doing, sitting here with me? Invisibility can be infectious, you know. It doesn't pay to breathe the same air as me. Remember what happened to the Christian man who put his beanie on the pavement. Stay with me long enough, some of it will rub off on you. Just like me, you will find yourself sitting down with all those fine words and loose prayers trapped in your mouth. You don't see the danger, and in some ways that is quite touching. Some might mistake it for courage.

18

You are curious to know if I have any adventures. I think you want my life here on the street as an invisible to be exciting. More exciting, perhaps, than your own life. I suspect your own life to be so dull, you must seek excitement in unlikely places such as this. I think you are mistaken. You are looking in the wrong place. Nothing sensational happens. If you're looking for stories, go with the drunks to the graveyard.

Things may happen here, on the street. Rain may suddenly fall from a sky that was blue a short moment ago. Someone may bring me a falafel or a pastry. A hundred dollar note may fall out of the sky. PC might set her pipe-cleaner creatures free to go their own way and wreak havoc. But adventures? They are for the visible. Those who glory in the world. Or the drunks who are always looking for fights. Plenty of adventure there. You could always climb mountains or do some white water rafting, or bungee jump off the harbour bridge. That's what people do for excitement in the visible world. They do it because they like to have stories to tell after they have done it. It is the stories that are important to them, to have something to tell people.

I don't have anything to tell people, because there is nothing to tell. There are no stories here, and certainly no heroics. Sometimes I see heroes walking past, but they are too heroic to take any interest in me, or even see me. I don't offer any opportunities for heroes to be heroes, which I think perhaps is lucky for me. They all have stories. Everybody has stories. That's all we are, just a bunch of stories.

For me, there is no narrative because there is no thread, no connecting tissue between this event and the next. The same street opens to the same street. The hubcaps fly away, and return. The skipping girl comes back to the ground. Two butts make a ciggie, Jinee says. There is no meat, only bone. Consider the unopened packet of cigarettes and the hundred-dollar note, both arriving within minutes of each other. That is strange but it is not a story. It doesn't add up to anything. It's just two events happening side-by-side. There is no hidden connection, nor any moral to be drawn. There is nothing you can do with it but say, wow, smoke the cigarettes and spend the money. When nothing happens, that's all that's happening.

But you, of course, want more... we have our own little supply and demand going here. Perhaps you see me as some sort of entertainment centre.

Alright then, I'll tell you one, and we'll see where it gets us.

Boy Blue was a generator of stories. I don't mean he told stories, I mean stories happened around him. Other people would get pulled in. That's because he was on the run, always on the lookout, always putting two and two together. Always trying to get home again.

Like the scarab beetle, he found himself in the wrong world, and he spent a lot of his time trying to find a way back. He told me that he wasn't really an invisible person, that he had a proper mother and father and family in his own world. A family and a home to live in. Quiet, shady streets to walk and parks to visit. In that world everybody lived in big houses and drove big cars and the sky was always blue and flowers grew along the roadside and people came and went without fear, with smiles on their faces and gifts in their hands. Everybody cared about everybody. Feasts were held on birthdays and deathdays, and elves rode around on bicycles without using their hands, singing arias. They could steer without touching the handlebars, he said.

He told us other things about his world too, which couldn't be true. About the man with the head of a fish, for example, who played the ukulele when the sun went down, and soldiers with the faces of dogs, and children who never went to school but played all day on soft, sandy beaches, and towers that turned into spaceships, and poets that painted the streets.

I decided he was too little to be able to distinguish real things from imagined things and things he had seen in books or comics. It all got scrambled up, maybe when he followed the cockroach trail to this world, to this dreary piece of street. Things came out of his mind and walked around. I think they chased him here, whatever they are, because sometimes he sees things others can't see. Once he pointed to an empty space, his face creased with terror. He followed it up the road, whatever it was, with this eyes and his pointing finger. I couldn't see it, and people passing walked through that space without apparently meeting any resistance. And yet if you looked hard enough you could almost make it out, an empty space moving up the street.

He said that things had followed him here, along the cockroach trail, and soon they would find him if he didn't move on. Perhaps you might find that exciting. Moving on was the important thing, he said. If you keep moving on, the world can't catch up with you. That's the trick. Perhaps there will come a time when his pursuers will not be able to see him. He will have moved on so often that there will be nothing more of him to see. Only in such absolute invisibility will he be able to find any safety.

19

One day he took me by the hand and urged me to follow him. I am always reluctant to leave my spot on the steps to the old bank, especially during the day. There are a host of invisibles ready to take my place, I'm sure. I have a plumb position here in front of the old bank, framed by Greek columns. Take the woman who sits opposite me on the other side of the road, for example. While she has a nice shop front, it is dingy and doubtless smelly compared to my nice open steps. And the grand green door behind me that never opens. I'm sure she must envy me. Were I to leave it for any length of time, I have no doubt that she would come across the road and take my place. Nobody would care, except maybe Jinee.

Despite all this, I did follow him. As soon as I got to my feet I became visible, even though people quickly looked the other way as soon as they saw me, in order to protect themselves. Some even make the sign of the cross as if to ward off evil. Like a pariah, an invisible person is supposed to stay that way. Any change of status is viewed with great suspicion. One may become invisible and provoke little more than the lift of an eyebrow or a pious sentiment, but to go the other way, and reappear again, is looked upon as bad form, in fact socially irresponsible. If you go invisible, you should at least have the decency to stay that way, that's the implication. Unless, of course, you reappear in a tailor-made suit with five hundred dollar shoes. Then both eyebrows go up and a smile appears, and you are greeted like the prodigal son.

All this made me uncomfortable, but I pressed on, followed Boy Blue along the street, past the falafel take-away, past the cake shop with the coffee smells, past the tourist traps with their fluffy cuddly icons and nationalistic t-shirts, past the clothing shops with their vacant mannequins and smiling sales staff, past the Korean restaurant that doesn't open until 4pm and where I once, briefly, sat down, past another invisible person who looked up at me without hope, until we came to a small side alley. Every city has them, these anonymous little openings which might have interesting little shops or holes-in-the-wall where some craft is offered. The first thing I see is a man sitting at his open window repairing a watch. He has lots of complicated little instruments. A little further in there is the side entry of a bakery. An open door offers a glimpse of ovens and men and women in white jackets. A little further along there is a tiny opening where a woman is selling donuts for half the price they cost on the main street. She only has room to display six donuts. She looks up at me without interest as we go past.

As we continue I noticed other changes, subtle at first. The sound of the city changed. Every city has its own distinctive voice. Just as the sound of the sea changes with the shape of the coastline, the sound of a city will change with the shape of the sky and the land around, whether there are hills around about or not and so on. I have become accustomed to the sound of our city, its background hum. Because the main street slopes from the ridge to the port below, much of the sound I hear flows downward, from above, with the prevailing wind, and vanishes away as it passes me. I have grown accustomed to that imbalance of sound, and naturally enough, have ceased to notice it.

Following Boy Blue down the grey alley I felt the balance of sound shift. It was no longer flowing down but eddying about, as if all the land around had become flat and the wind had lost its way. At the same time, or shortly after, the sound of voices changed too, shifting frequency, it seemed. The sound of people talking and laughing and calling to one another across bounded spaces might be likened to the sound of birds in a forest. But what if every bird was replaced by another of a different species? The sound of the song would change. And that's what happened here. The song of the city changed as if the throats of the singers had altered, as if a different air passed over their vocal chords.

The little businesses each side began to change, too. Instead of someone selling coffee or donuts from their windows, a man was heating some tea in a beaker over a Bunsen burner. In another, a woman was folding clothes. I couldn't quite work out what her business was. Did people bring her clothes to fold? How silly was that. Perhaps she had just ironed them, but there was no iron in sight. Perhaps she did laundry, but there was no washing machine in sight.

The walls too were becoming taller, darker. The alleyway was becoming narrower, the strip of sky above more remote, like a length of tape holding the walls upright. I tried to recall the street layout of this part of our city. As far as I knew, we should have come to a major road, one that ran parallel to our Main Street. At the same time signs of economic activity began to fade. There were fewer doorways and windows. Muffled sounds came from behind the walls like distant engines thumping. Suddenly it seemed that I was on a ship. I could feel the ground vibrating faintly beneath me.

I stopped and looked at Boy Blue. I didn't like this so much, I told him. I felt like I had travelled a very long distance. He didn't say anything. He's no great talker, Boy Blue. I sometimes wonder if he has ever learned properly. But he encouraged me on with smiles and gestures.

We continued until we came to a long dark wall familiar from my dreams. There were no little teashops or hole in the wall donut shops or anything in this wall. It was long and featureless and seemed to go on forever, as far as the eye could see. There was not even any graffiti. I understood that this wall marked some kind of incomprehensible boundary. That it wasn't really a wall, not in the proper sense. I only saw it that way, because that is the only way I could see it, the only way my eye could represent it. Whatever lay on the other side of it is something I could never understand.

On the other side of that wall lay Boy Blue's home.

I felt, then, like a very tiny little cockroach indeed. A blind cockroach feeling its way along through a world beyond its comprehension. Imagine a cockroach crawling around inside a guitar. No matter how thoroughly it crawls about it can have no idea of what a guitar is. It might even brush the strings and still have no idea. That's what I was doing. I was brushing the strings. I could feel the vibration but had no idea what the song was.

As with any other creature, a cockroach likes familiar haunts. There are lots of highways and byways on Insect Street but none of them are like this. Insect Street is a busy place with lots of scurrying to and fro. The wall was frightening for the cockroach for there were no cracks in it, no little fissures formed by the weather, nothing upon which to gain any purchase. Nowhere to hide. It was as smooth and impenetrable as ice yet as warm as flesh. It might have been the skin of some unknown creature, the carapace of a monstrous beetle more like it. The mile high cockroach.

The more I thought about it, the smaller I became. It seemed impossible that I could ever get back to my familiar street and my spot on the steps of the old bank, Jinee and the skipping girl.

I became so small the air grew thick. Not darkness as of night, but greyness as of smog. The air was smeared with soot.

I looked around for Boy Blue, but he was not there. Or rather, he was there but was someone else. He had shed his cockroach self to reveal a tall being as thin as a thistle. He had gold eyes that shone like coins in a cup, and blue skin the colour of the ocean on a bright day. I gathered that this was why we were here. That he had to bring me here, to the edge of the world, to show me his true form, what he looked like when he was not being invisible.

He wanted me to know, to see him like this. I have no idea why. Perhaps he felt grateful to me for allowing him a place on my precious steps, to hide him from any passing eyes. Hunters. Perhaps he felt obligated to me. Perhaps he had even felt, for a moment, that Jinee and me and him did in fact make a little family.

I had no idea why he should take on the cloak of invisibility and hang with us on the street. I sensed that he once lived on the other side of this wall, if it had another side, and one day he just found himself on the wrong side. Easy enough to do. A little displacement is all it takes. But none of this speculation was of much use to me. I was here, stranded in some kind of no-man's-land without knowing how to get back, and the transformed Boy Blue showed no sign of turning back.

I began to despair. There was nothing here. Even the changed sounds of the city had faded. As the air grew thicker, the world grew more silent. The blue being had a mouth but it was only for smiling. I understood he didn't want to shrink back into what he was on the street, a scared urchin with funny coloured hair.

I wanted out. A cockroach could die in a place like this, very easily. A great foot from the sky is all it would take.

I turned to try to find my way back on my own, but there was nothing except more dark wall, which had begun by now to feel like the walls of a prison with me on the inside. The wall became a Moebius strip that twists about on itself and offers a surface with only one side and only one boundary. A cockroach could scuttle around that single surface forever and never get any closer to the other side.

Surely, Boy Blue did not bring me here to die.

At that moment I heard a familiar sound, although far off. It took me a second to recognize it. It was the sound of a skipping rope hitting hard pavement. Swish-tick, swish-tick, tickety-swish. I could have cried with relief. At the same time I wondered how I could be hearing it when all the other sounds of the world had faded to nothing, even the blast of car horns and the grinding roar of trucks, the whoop and clamour of sirens. The tolling of iron bells. There was nothing of that. Just that one sound, changing as it grew nearer. Swish-slap, swish-slap.

And along with the swish-slap the familiar undertone. The little light voice of a child playing.

Can't get a red bird, blue bird'll do.
Can't get a red bird, blue bird'll do.
Can't get a red bird, blue bird'll do.
Skip to my Lou, my darlin!

I looked at the blue being. It was laughing, stars sparkling in its mouth. But something was wrong with the blue being. Like a bad phone line, it was starting to break up.

Can't get a dollar so a penny will do.
Can't get a dollar so a penny will do.
Can't get a dollar so a penny will do.
Skip to my Lou, my darlin!

I looked around for the skipping girl and couldn't see her anywhere. But the grayness was beginning to clear from the air. The blue being's mouth had turned into a strip of sky in which real stars could be seen impossibly far off. The dark wall began to fade as the air cleared. The sounds of the city began to seep back, first in waves and then more steadily.

The quiver in the ground beneath my feet subsided and the city began to reassemble itself around me. Here were the walls of the alley we had gone down. There was the smell of sugar coffee from the donut shop. And the sound of human voices calling to each other. And the insect hum of Insect Street. The human world was returning, slowly, piece by piece, like a jig-saw puzzle. The blue being was changing too, diminishing in size, slowly returning to human form, Boy Blue with the scared face. The boy who would hide from the sun. The shapeshifter.

Apparently this transformation, so reassuring to me, was a frightening experience for him. He didn't want to go back to the street, to the steps of the old bank, to the passing parade of indifferent humanity, to his life as a homeless urchin. This now rapidly fading dark wall, which seemed to merge back into the city rather than disappear, as if the city were its disguise, was as close as the Boy Blue could get to his home, his home beyond the wall. For a moment he looked desperate, as if he had to hold back the very forces of time and space, which, of course, was impossible.

I saw the skipping girl first. There she was, rising and falling as her rope whirled about her. Until the ground materialized beneath her, she seemed to rise and fall in mid air. I could hear the sound of her rope as it swung through the air, whoop, whoop. Around her, bits of my familiar world pieced themselves together. The street behind, up which a bus was lumbering, the shop fronts across the road, where my mirror woman sat in her deep doorway. People walking back and forward as if they had somewhere real to go.

The vibration in the ground disappeared as the familiar pavement came up to meet my feet. I was standing, not far from my steps to the old bank, people walking politely around me. I wasn't far from where we'd started. Nobody saw us appear there except the skipping girl. She was looking at us and smiling. I smiled back. One of the few moments we had acknowledged each other - the invisible may see each other, but they often pretend not to.

In the moment that we exchanged smiles I had the feeling that the skipping girl had saved us, or at least me. With her whirling rope she had summoned us back to the world, transported us on its blurred flight like a magic carpet.

I took a quick look around to see the alley down which Boy

Blue and I had ventured. I knew it was there somewhere, between one doorway and another, between the tourist traps and
the coffee shops.

Without delay I returned to the steps. My steps. No one had
occupied them in my absence, thank goodness, although the
fat man with the mop of hair had moved closer, finding a spot
by the bus-stop. Jinee wasn't there, although I could see her
approaching in the distance, her head bowed as she scanned
the pavement for cigarette butts.

In that moment I could have loved the world and everything in it.

20

So... my perfect listener. Your mind is whizzing around like the
skipping girl's rope. I'm afraid I can't do the jumps for you; my
legs don't work that way. I never was great at obedience.

Perhaps you realize how little interested I am in paying you
back for some imagined favour, what little sense of obligation
I feel where you are concerned. It's not that I don't appreciate
the hearty beef sandwiches and the hot tea out of the thermos.
You think you are very kind. I understand that.

I advised you from the start that it was not a real story, or
adventure of any kind. Why, you are saying, he might never
have moved more than a little distance from his precious steps.
Those steps that lead nowhere but which are the nearest thing

he has to a home. Nothing really happened, you are saying. Just some thoughts and impressions passing through his head. After all, when real things happen people are changed. People are changed by the world and by the stories they live though. I have not changed at all. I am as invisible as ever. I have not moved an inch, and I have not changed a hair on the head of the world. I told you there was no adventure here. I gave you fair warning. You can take your disappointment down the road where somebody might appreciate it.

So let me ask you this. You think I am so bored I make up stories and incidents to pass the time of day and fend off boredom, but what would you do if you didn't come and talk to me each day? Walk up and down the street as if you had somewhere to go? Sit in that café over there and drink coffee and watch other people do the same? Can it be that your life is more boring than mine? To seek me out to make your time more easily passing. You read into my situation all kind of fascinating features and aspects, which you go away and assiduously write down, I'm sure, because you have a problem with forgetting.

What you don't appreciate is that you will forget it anyway, after you have written it down. In fact, writing it down makes it possible for you to happily forget about it - you have written it down so why should you remember? So your writing is an act of forgetfulness. When you have finished it you will put it away with great relief, and move on to something else. Hopefully something with a little more excitement. You know, passion, danger, and being on the edge of your seat.

There's nothing like that here, just a grubby homogeneity. I'm sure you can do better. The woman across the street looks like she might have stories to tell. PC could tell you a few stories if you could get her talking. As it is, it's the pipe-cleaner creatures that have all the adventures and get to poke children's eyes out.

If anybody else reads your notes, they too will have permission to forget. Forgetfulness is an essential aspect of contentment, depending on what it is you are forgetting. I think that before you came to me, you couldn't forget me. You were one of the many passersby, one of the passing parade, but something stuck. I know this because I remember your legs. You always slowed down a little, because you were observing me. I always notice the people who notice me. Perhaps you didn't quite realize that noticing me was the first step on the road to invisibility.

When I first saw you, I think I mistook you for another kind of walker, those who are pretending to have somewhere to go. This pretense gives them a purpose in life. They put on their best clothes. They polish their shoes. They carry a bag or briefcase. They walk up and down quite briskly sometimes as if they were off to some important meeting or appointment. Their legs make important movements through the air, just like the real movers and shakers of the world. Sometimes they will swing their arms as if they were marching. Sometimes I can only pick them because they walk past me several times, going one way then the other, or one way over and over as they walk around and around the block. They are trying to fool people that they have real things to do and that life has some meaning for them. They are the real sad-sacks.

But as it turned out, you were not like that. You made several passes, it is true, but you were scoping out the territory, summoning the courage to come up and sit by me and start up a conversation. But you never made your agenda clear, never came clean as to what you were really doing. Even now I have to guess. I'm only guessing, for example, that you will write any of this down. I only think you will because you have a special way of listening. You are listening to remember so you can write to forget. You have that kind of busy mind. A nosy-parker.

That's so complicated. I like to think, at least, that life as an invisible is much simpler. All I need to know is if you have the price of a meal in your pocket, or if the wind will blow cold tonight. So your desire to expose me, if that's what it is, is doomed to failure because there is nothing to expose. On examination, you find the invisible has no substance after all, no hidden depths, no anthropological oddities to amuse you or your readers - if you have readers. I exist, but only through negation. There is nothing for you to grasp. Go home, if you have one. Lead a simple life. Eat when you're hungry and drink when you're dry. Love someone if love comes your way. Write for your perfect reader if you must, but leave me out of it.

I've done nothing, which is about the limit of my powers.

You put money in my plate as if you were buying my time

or my favour. All this was just to keep away the dead that keep following you around…. oh, you didn't know I could see them… you are not the only one, you know. Plenty of people have the dead trailing along behind them. The dead get bored too, you know. They have nothing better to do than follow live people around.

There's a story in that, surely.

21

I wouldn't want you to harbour any illusions. Because I am here today doesn't mean that I'll be here tomorrow. Just as a coin may disappear into thin air before it reaches my enamel bowl, so I too will disappear, fade from view even as you are watching me.

God will snatch me out of the air.

The atoms of my feet are beginning to jiggle. Sometimes the street fades away as if it were in some old newsreel. I can tell you this because I know you will pass no judgments, and that you understand that everything that happens in the land of the invisible is momentary. There is no accumulation here, which is what Pablo found out. No moment can be piled onto the one proceeding to accumulate meaning or history. It's twenty to eleven all the way down. The bankroll in your shoe keeps shrinking. You know deep in your heart that one day you will come here and the steps will be empty. Or only Jinee will be here and she won't know what you are talking about. Or only the skipping girl will be here and you will hear nothing but the tickety-scrape of her rope on the pavement.

History is not possible for invisibles. There's nothing to shore up the self against time. Time and tide wait for no man, isn't that the saying? So one day I will be gone, and it will truly be as if I had never been. A room might hold the imprint of a person for a time, houses get haunted and so on, but not so an empty step on a public street. It holds nothing except the chill of the night or the warmth of a day.

My regulars will quickly forget their aberrant behaviour, and you, even you, will have to relegate me to the status of an occasional thought. A memory that will soon seem like a daydream and then like nothing at all. You may see the empty steps and something may tug at your mind, lightly, but that will be all.

That is the way it is with us. We drop out of sight. That is what we are supposed to do.

We move on.

It is likely that some other invisible will take my place on the steps of the old bank. They won't remain empty for long. It can get crowded in the shadow of the dark walls.

I know that you think we have some kind of social significance. Even you. You who should know better. That's just a kind of academic romanticism. I have no more social significance than some random piece of plastic you might stuff into your rubbish. Would you pick out some ripped corner of some insignificant plastic wrapping and make a study of it, describe its contours, map its randomly jagged edges, examine it from every angle for its peculiarities, submit it to your magnifying glass? Why would you bother?

I think you want to pin me down, like a butterfly in a case, expose my soft underbelly to the world - all with the best intentions, of course. Here is an underbelly the world might admire, after a fashion, before moving on. In that admiration you will, momentarily, exist. The expression is to 'bathe in admiration' and it is an apt one, although you will always maintain that you didn't do it to gain admiration and some people might believe you. But they will never believe that a cockroach is a butterfly.

You want to know about my history, my past, where I was born and went to school and what I used to eat for breakfast and what the colour of my mother's eyes were. More than that, what I'm thinking about as people walk past, what I feel when the sun goes down and the buildings turn into canyons, where I get my words from, my winter coat. Next it will be my bowel habits and my sex life.

When you probe into these things I feel empty, because you have still not understood, even when I speak as plain as day. Over and over, you keep searching the empty room, looking for the past that never existed. I was never born, I never went to school, I had nothing for breakfast, and my mother's eyes were born of a fish. I keep my bowel habits to a minimum and, truly, you don't want to know about my sex life.

I tell you these things but you continue to speak as if I have not spoken. Luckily, I am accustomed to that. It goes with the territory. I say what people want me to say or nothing at all. I am permitted a little gratitude for the benevolence of others, but not much more than that. More would be unseemly. And to be unseemly is to be noticed.

I am sorry if you have wasted your time on the basis of false assumptions. I don't want to be a disappointment to you. I was afraid right from the start that I was just a project of yours, and that your perfect listening was part of a larger and less perfect agenda. I didn't want to think that, because it somehow made your listening less than perfect. I'm sorry to rain on your parade, as people say when they are not sorry at all, and to disenchant you, but what you are looking for is not to be found, not here on Invisible Street. You are looking in the wrong place. I understand how frustrating it must be for you. Just when it seems that you are on the edge of it... that it will shortly come into sight... the goalposts move and it eludes you once more.

There may even come a time when I might have to drive you away, beef sandwiches and all. I might have to tell you that you cannot dress me up me with words, like a ventriloquist's doll, and with those words turn me back into something visible again. That won't happen. Rather, these words themselves will become invisible, as if you have written them with invisible ink, as the world goes on its merry way. The mystics have told you that you can stop the world, but that doesn't seem very likely.

Perhaps I am right, and underneath it all you are like the

Christian. You are planning my redemption. Salvation by words. By redeeming me you redeem yourself. That's a joke… I'll say to you what I said to him, it's all just a load of silly nonsense. Your precious redemption is simply more denial. I am not looking for redemption, I am looking for a coin or two, thank you, bless you, may you have a great day.

22

All good things come to an end, I have heard.

I don't know if this has been a good thing or not.

See those men in white overalls with the ladders and the scaffolding, and the rolls of white plastic, unloading them and laying them along the side of the street. Shortly, they will be erecting it in order to give the old bank façade a facelift. They don't want it to look too grimy for the tourists. They don't care about a few beggars hanging out around McDonalds or Bar B Q Duck, but the bank façade must get its spit and polish. Since they will be sequestering off the steps from the street by a wall of plastic, soon, without acknowledging me, they will be pressing me to move on. So I will press on.

Coins always flash brighter on the other side of the street. Perhaps I will cross over and join the woman there who is my mirror. She has a nice little spot in her deep, abandoned doorway. Maybe there is room for two.

I have a gift I could take her, something to sweeten the way.

A hundred dollars in her beanie would sweeten the way.

Even if I were to disappear from these steps right in front of everybody, only a few would notice and even fewer would pause to wonder. A miracle can quickly turn into a trick of light. Somebody might pick up my bowl and throw it in the rubbish. You can find evidence of this sort of civic mindedness in our general populace. One of my regulars might find themselves at the end of the day with a stray coin in their pocket. The skipping girl might miss a step. Nothing else would happen. Nobody would notice any difference. The invisible who replaces me on the steps will be indistinguishable from me. We are a mass. We wear the ghost of a common face.

And if I were to magically reappear somewhere, further down the street, in some likely doorway, nobody would be amazed. They might assume I had been there all along, that they'd just missed seeing me. That is, if they thought about it at all. They certainly wouldn't see any miraculous resurrection.

For you it might be different. You might be talking to me one moment to find me gone in the next. Turn away for a second distracted by something and the world changes. Turn back and I'm not there. You'll never be quite sure if I became visible to you through your own efforts or virtue, or if I allowed myself to become visible to you for no particular reason at all.

We down here on Insect Street have our pride. We don't want to reveal all our secrets.

While you are, and must remain, my most perfect listener, I believe I am an aberration in your life. At least it tickles me to think so. You visible people are always on a mission of some kind. People are made for each other's missions. I see lots of knights in shining armour and damsels in distress in search of one another, although the damsels are not exactly damsels and the men are not exactly knights. I have witnessed such meetings on the street. The joy of discovery. The taste of saliva. A burst of sunshine.

I am the aberration in your mirror. I sit here and wait for you to come. Eventually they all come, angry, reconciled or sheepish. In the shiny hubcap, our figures merge and become one. In some fashion you don't understand, I am made for your quest. You know the old saying - if I didn't exist you would have to invent me. Unfortunately I can't reciprocate the favour. I'm sure we already understand this. The invisible have no mission. We are powerless. We are written in invisible ink. I couldn't invent you, even if I needed you. In truth, I can barely conceive the perfect listener.

Here come the security guards. Their dark green uniforms are almost the colour of the old bank door. It will be their job to keep an eye on the scaffolding overnight. Already they are casting glances in my direction, as if they were getting ready to actually see me. The workmen in white overalls are relaxed. Tomorrow they will erect the scaffolding. Their lives are cut and dried. The scaffolding will fit together, pipe into pipe; the hours will go the same way.

I will be in the wind, as they say. Moved on.

Sooner or later it gets to this. The sun goes down or the sun comes up. The tourists come to the end of their drinks. The last falafel, the last sunset on the harbour, the last hero. As they part ways they think, oh we will meet again tomorrow or next week or after the moon has a birthday. But there is no tomorrow or next week and the moon never has a birthday. That doesn't deter people. Without such comforts life would become intolerable. The tourists go back to their cruise ship. Oh, they are having the time of their lives. There is always one more drink, one more sunset on the harbour. One more invisible person fading into the stonework.

Sooner or later it gets back to this. Men arrive out of the morning twilight to erect scaffolding. They are going to scrub this tiny part of the world clean. Which means me. I get scrubbed, too. Scrubbed out with the graffiti. The world might sink into a cloud of unbeing, or burn up in heat death, but the old bank façade will stand staunch with a freshly scrubbed face. It's amazing what a bit of spit and polish will do.

I'd like to think that you might return one day, to this piece of street, and look around for me and Jinee and the skipping girl. We will be gone. I see you pausing for a moment, just a little mystified. What happened here, you wonder. Did you lose something, gain something? Did you see something... or get a piece of city grit in your eye? Was anybody ever here? Were you, at least for a time, a perfect listener?

You may wonder if you ever spent time talking to a cockroach, watching a hummingbird vibrate through worlds, or commiserating with a donkey because there aren't enough cigarettes in the world. But I am the one who is romanticizing now. It's easy enough to do. Even believing you to be a perfect listener is something of a folly on my part. My conceit, if you prefer. There are no perfect anybodies.

There's no such thing as a perfect invisible either. Little patches will show, here and there. A little bit of me might leak into the world. A little bit of homelessness. I can't prevent that. To be perfectly invisible would be to be perfectly dead. A little stumble here and there, a little awkwardness, soon puts a stop to that. To be imperfect is to be alive.

For you I will always remain an unfinished piece of work. Very imperfect. It will niggle at you, but you will never know what it all adds up to. What it means. You will go on asking the wrong questions and curse life for not having the answers. One day, perhaps, you will find your own invisibility. Meet it on your own terms. Negotiate it with your own instruments. Find your own set of steps. Park your arse in a public place and turn your other cheek.

There is a date. It exists in time. You can put a ring around it. You can put it through the wringer. You can't change the fact of it. It might come out all wrinkled and crinkled but underneath it is just the same. It is a date. It is a moment of conjunction. You will arrive at that date the way a passenger arrives at a station, complete with suitcase. You will be transported there. You will glance at your watch to make sure it's twenty to eleven. It's all about time and coincidence. It's all about putting a good face on things as the station approaches. It's all about checking clocks to make sure time is operating properly. That you will arrive at the date.

It's all about moving on.

As the cheerful workmen and the security guards confer, I bow my head. I wait for the executioners axe. I wait for my head to go tumbling into my begging bowl. God might pluck my head out of the air before it can hit the bowl, and restore it to my neck. He'd better be quick. I feel the icy touch at the back of my neck. Already the world is falling head over heels as my head tumbles towards the bowl.

It's easy for you. You can reach your hand out and scratch the sky. You can start from scratch. Anything is possible for you. You have home. Home is the magic scratch word. Home makes the heart a hero. You can breathe now! Be glad! We invisibles are, by definition, homeless. That is, houses stopped recognizing us. Doors shut with an iron certainty, windows turned their faces away. Invisibility is our home. Insect Street is the place. It offers no protection from the elements, not even from the judgments of others. And not from workmen and security guards and nosy parkers, all of whom have homes.

Hunger is a one way street. You can see it in the hubcaps. You can hear it sing in the orbit of the skipping rope. A skipping hope. A bus kneels to take on a crowd of commuters, all going home. See, my humble enamel bowel is still out, still open to receive. It's all battered and worn but game for another round. Being a cockroach, I don't have very much to offer other than my hunger.

Here it is. You may drop a coin into the begging bowl. Two if you wish. The heavy ones sound better. A note will make it to the right place quite silently.

Thank you very much. Have a nice night.

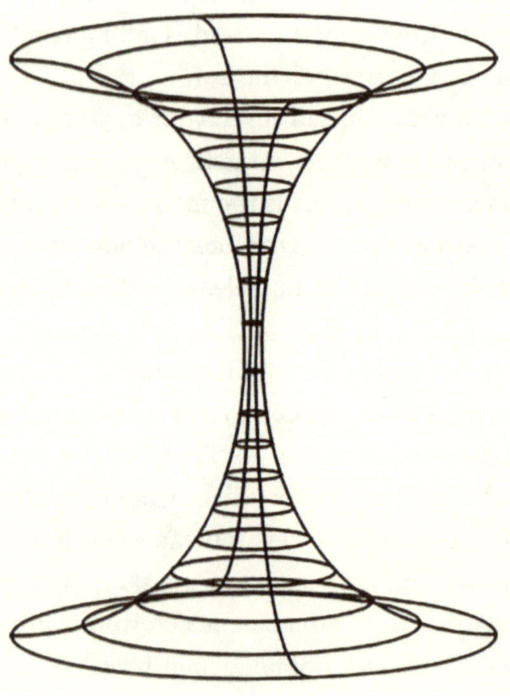

It's fitting that your wandering has brought you to this little corner of the world, this single spot on the map. On that map, an arrow points to you. You are here, where you find yourself. Think, for a moment, of all the other places you could be. I bet most of them are better than this, standing in front of me, a shabby old head-stone, wondering what you're doing here. As I said, I'm not much to look at; what you see is what you get. It's what you came for; that's the thing. That's what we all need to know. Everybody comes for something, even if just to play on the grass with the children or join the picnic.

Headstone

Other books by Mike Johnson

Novels
Hold My Teeth While I Teach You To Dance, 99% Press, Auckland.
Travesty. Titus Books, Auckland.
Stench. Hazard Press, Christchurch.
Counterpart. Harper Collins, Sydney.
Dumb Show. Longacre Press, Dunedin.
Lethal Dose. Hard Echo Press, Auckland.
Antibody Positive. Hard Echo Press, Auckland.
Lear: The Shakespeare Company Plays Lear at Babylon. Hard Echo Press,
Auckland.

Shorter Fiction
Back in the Day: Tales from NZ's Own Paradise Island. 99% Press, Auckland.
Foreigners. Penguin Books, Auckland.

Poetry
To Beatrice: Where We Crossed the Line. Pie Press, Auckland.
Vertical Harp: The Selected Poems of Li He. Titus Books, Auckland.
Treasure Hunt. Auckland University Press, Auckland.
Standing Wave. Hard Echo Press, Auckland.
From a Woman in Mt Eden Prison & Drawing Lessons. Hard Echo Press,
Auckland.
The Palanquin Ropes. Voice Press, Wellington.

Non Fiction
Angel of Compassion. TP Press, Auckland.

Children's Fiction
Taniwha. Illustrated by Jennifer Rackham. Beansprout Press, Auckland.

'After finishing Mike Johnson's *Travesty*, and re-reading his previous novels and poetry, I have come to the conclusion that, with it, he has achieved the epitome or culmination of something. He has achieved a kind of 'worldmaking' – to borrow American philosopher Nelson Goodman's famous term – that confirms his position as one of New Zealand's most important fiction writers.
Judy Dalgleish, 'Half Way House of the Soul', Landfall.

'One of the most innovative, original and fearless writers I know.'
Witi Ihimaera

'Mike Johnson is the most underrated of all living New Zealand authors. Sometimes gothic, sometimes lyrical, sometimes both at once, his output over the past three decades has been extraordinary. Yet much of his fiction and most of his poetry has slipped by, barely reviewed.'
Iain Sharp on *The Vertical Harp: Selected Poems of Li He*, Sunday Star-Times.

'*Dumb Show* is a triumph... It's a rare item, a fully sustained poetic novel… Johnson is a writer who always tests the borders of fiction.'
Gerry Webb, Quote Unquote, 1997

'It's not often that we get a local novel of such verbal texture.' David Dowling, Landfall, *Lear - the Shakespeare Company plays Lear at Babylon*

Headstone

Mike Johnson

99% Press

Published by 99% Press,
an imprint of Lasavia Publishing Ltd.
Auckland, New Zealand
www.lasaviapublishing.com

ISBN: 978-0-473-39766-1

But since you think't an easy thing
To mount above the moon,
Of your own fiddle take a spring
And dance when you have done.

1

Welcome to my turf.

It seems that you have arrived somewhere.

Better late than never, as they say!

It's not much, I know. Here we make do with very little. A simple salad made of weeds, patches of light and a stony path or two. Throw in a slim-necked vase, a few flowers, and an adventurous spider. Listen hard enough and you may hear the laughter of children playing. It comes and goes; sometimes you hear them, sometimes you don't.

Step right up. Take turns if you wish. Make a wish if you wish. I'm open to all comers, the long and the short and the tall. I'm not much to look at, but I've got staying power.

And I don't change my tune halfway through the song.

Bless 'em all! All comers are welcome. We make no distinctions on the ground of race, creed or colour. And money doesn't cut it around here either. You can arrive flashing your wealth but the grave is like a very empty street. Nobody is watching.

Nobody is taking notes or clicking tickets. This is the land of the headstone, and nobody gets turned away.

I'm happy to meet you.

It's fitting that your wandering has brought you to this little corner of the world, this single spot on the map. On that map, an arrow points to you. *You are here*, where you find yourself. Think, for a moment, of all the other places you could be. I bet most of them are better than this, standing in front of me, a shabby old headstone, wondering what you're doing here. As I said, I'm not much to look at; what you see is what you get. It's what you came for; that's the thing. That's what we all need to know. Everybody comes for something, even if just to play on the grass with the children or join the picnic.

You're not the only one. Everywhere you look people are wandering about as if they were tourists, getting an eyeful, checking out the flowers and the headstones and each other. Some are planning to buy, looking to move in full-time when the time comes. They aim to secure their plot. They look at the epitaphs or feel them with their fingers. Sometimes words aren't real until you can touch them, trace them, push your fingers into the cracks between them. People have different ways of making sure of the world.

Most come here for a little grief. There's comfort in grief, people forget that. Even you might grieve. That's not so strange. Everybody likes to feel connected to their feelings. A few tears do a lot of work before going home for the night, bunch of flowers in hand.

There's not enough grief to go around, apparently, for all the tragedies of the world. The pool of tears is drying up under a hard sun. We can't dedicate every moment to crying. Already there are huge, untapped sources of suffering; soon the beasts will come to feed. I hope there is a lot of laughter in your picnic bucket, along with your ever-hopeful bread and wine.

A lot of good lives are being wasted, being gobbled up and spat out. I get the homeless coming to me from Lonely Avenue with their grief in their hands looking for a place to rest their heads, but I'm not offering any comforts. I make for a pretty stony pillow. It's not my job to take all these people in. I'm not equipped for it. You come to me, that's a different thing. Like me, you're supposed to be here. We tolerate the living for the sake of the dead. We don't let our grief go to waste.

If you have come looking for grief, you've come to the right place. We're specialists here. Grief, you might say, is our business. Joy sleeps rough at night along with the street people, while here grief gets the five-star treatment. We have angels in attendance, weeping stone tears. We have asphodels and cypresses, the latter always striving towards heaven. We have trimmed lawns and obedient roses, and little fairy-tale paths with white stones. We have spiders that can spin their webs to the moon and a cockroach that visits us from another dimension.

You might say we are the go-to place for the connoisseurs of grief. They will come here on a Sunday afternoon with their children and their tissues, some with picnic baskets. They can always find some tears in the grass, the long grass or the short grass. Sometimes I see them crawling about, collecting translucent tears.

One well-dressed lady came by with a little red velvet box into which she placed all the stray and uncollected tears she could find. I think she got her fair share. I imagine her going home to her quietly expensive house in the suburbs, opening her little red box and gloating over the tears within, stroking them, each little pearl testifying to one authentic moment of existence.

Some people feel awkward when they see me, or pass me by, but I have no begging bowl or outstretched palm. In fact, I don't ask for anything. I'm content to let the days go by along with the people, the visitors, the day trippers – and those like you. When you consider me, there's not much to look at. Just a few words scratched on stone. You don't even have to read them to know what they are. You can pass on by, and it won't make any difference to me or the clouds above or the days scudding by. The words will still be there, facing outward, a little worn around the edges but still good to go.

A familiar name.

2

Apparently I have a following among the flowers, lilies especially. Lilies are seductive. They are all flower, all curve. Their nakedness is the nakedness of memory. Their contours hold the secret.

But it doesn't have to be lilies. I get all kinds of flowers, a great colourful array. You could say that flowers are my sky. People like to bring fresh cut flowers and put them at my feet to worship me and die. And that's what the blooms do. They stay upright in my shadow until the last possible moment. Then they surrender.

Flowers work for their tears. They work hard at their colours. They work for their homecoming, for their day in the sun. Nothing else says it like flowers. Their pollen is sweetest at the centre; that's an open secret. You can't go wrong with fresh cut flowers, not for immediate effect. You can always make a pretty arrangement of them in your slender-necked vase, set them up before me as if at a window, where they can nod in the breeze and impress passers-by.

They have a job to do. They have a fragrance to surrender, an image to maintain for as long as possible. You can say it with flowers. Here today, gone tomorrow. Cut flowers live on borrowed time just like everybody. They have to ration their fragrance. Slowly their gaze heads for the earth. Half in life, half in death, they go on blooming to the very last possible moment. It is the faith of flowers that people love.

Lilies, open to the world with their cool, slender curves are one thing, roses quite another. Roses are secretive creatures. They hold it all in. You can see them growing all around here; people keep them like pets. There is a tenderness in the heart of a rose. You can feel it burning brightly in your chest. It burns without consuming the flesh, but that's just a party trick. It's all about memory. People come here to seek out forgetfulness. Memory becomes a battlefield where names are forgotten or too dearly remembered. Memory becomes a house no longer inhabited. Even the ghosts have laid down their arms. Memory is an arrangement of flowers in a mossy jar on a windowsill. They have a fine view of the world from the window, and greet all comers equally. Since they remember, you are able to forget. It's a fair deal. You come by every week or every month with a fresh set of flowers in order to renew your forgetfulness. The freshest flowers remember best. They say the loudest hello to the past.

Some memories take a long time to die, and need lots of flowers, fields of them – not just a few wilting in a jar for the convenience of spiders. It's not long before the flowers become the only mourners left, their heads bowing in the wind. Their vigil doesn't end when everybody has gone home to a meal and glass of wine. They release memories to the open air as they fade. They colour the air with pictures of a life. Primary colours. A dab of red, a dab of blue. That's a bit of a life smudged onto the world, with all the other lives.

Memories fold themselves away as night comes on, as the bedrolls unroll. They veil their secrets. Like flowers, they grow old and tired. If you don't use them, you lose them. The neural pathways fade. That is as it should be. Forgetting is important. A dog pees on a headstone. Does anybody remember? Only the headstone.

And a forget-me-not that caught the dribble.

3

It's all about memory. You come here to seek out your memories. To renew them. To refresh them with fragrances. To gather them in from the cold. All the grief and forgetfulness you need are to be found in memories. Yet memories are a double-edged sword, even for a saint. They don't all come redolent with the odour of sanctity.

Perhaps it is your memories that have killed these blooms, not their severed stems or their bent wills or their love of song. It's odd, isn't it, how some memories will come back, return like ghosts from the graveyard on the fragrance of lilies, seemingly stronger than ever, whispering stories, always stories.

You bring your posy to the headstone. You lower your head in devotion. Words pass through your lips. Your breath tickles your throat. You leave the flowers in good faith. It's time to move on; there's a fresh veil of tears ahead. But still, forgetting doesn't always work. It's not a quick fix or sure-fire remedy. Someone has to pay. Some memories come back even stronger from their airing in the world. They quiver with colour, and are moist with perfume. They are in search of flowers, grief and forgetfulness.

As they give up their memories, you recover them. A memory has its own smell. Aromas rule. The essence of fragrance.

Some come from the earth, some from the sky; some come in the day, some come at night. Every hour, every moment, has its particular fragrance. Its own particular shifting winds.

Some come out of the past, and some lie in wait for you. The whole point about a fragrance is that it is elusive. A good fragrance plays hide and seek with the world. It is a tease. One moment it is there in your nostrils, measurable, tangible molecules, the next moment it is somewhere else, in some other place. The labouring heart struggles to keep up. Fragrances are good at leaving memories behind, but can't be pinned down or cornered. Theirs is the dominion of air. Smell it as often as you can, you can't take it with you. Fragrances of the earth will return to the earth; fragrances of the sky will dissipate into thin air. A fragrance has a body but doesn't have a shape. That is not a fragrance standing by your side right now. That is something else.

Something we haven't talked about yet.

I talk of flowers and fragrances because that's where we meet. These are the crossroads, where the fragrances of sky and earth conjoin, and where, in the long run, the body itself may be seen as a fragrance, momentary and miraculous.

Call it the flagrance of fragrance.

4

It's a brave flower that's still there in the morning ready to say hello and salute the sun. All night long, it holds the image of light within its folded petals. That's a memory too.

There's a spider, a shy black one, who likes to climb the stems and fashion webs out of memories and forgetfulness. She weaves the silk threads that hold the world together, slung between the brave flowers and my rough shadow. The spider has not yet put in an appearance. It's early days. The flowers still shake their darling buds; the web shakes the sky. The sky still sings its song of violet and blue. The children have not yet arrived, although you can hear the sound of them. Your feet crunch on the gravel path. The sound reassures you – momentarily. It's the sound of the world rubbing against the world.

Here comes the shiny black spider now. She clambers up out of forgetfulness, and crawls into the web to seek out the heart of space. She's not surprised that the web is still intact. Her legs know where to go. Her body remembers. She is the weaver of worlds.

She hears the crunch of gravel, and goes very still.

There is time – and then here isn't.

5

The spider is a lone creature, unlike the cockroach. The cockroach comes here from another world, squeezing between the interstices of time and space. This cockroach comes from a busy street. If you listen hard enough to its scratchings you can hear the sounds of engines, the wheels of industry turning. That sound is a long way from here, a long way from the sighing of the cypress tree and the bubbly sound of children.

It is generally thought that the dead prefer peace and quiet, a little seclusion, but actually it's the living that need these things. The dead don't care. Nor does the cockroach, the harbinger of silence. The cockroach's great indifference is its strength. Its hard, shiny carapace makes it impervious to the world. I've seen this one crawl through the spider's web as if it weren't there.

It's easy to understand why people react to the sight of a cockroach. If you see one there will be many somewhere nearby. They swarm in from other dimensions like creatures from outer space. I've seen them crawl out of the dreams of the dead.

You'll get used to them. They mean no harm. Like the spider, like all the little hard-backed, insect tears, they live in my shadow. You may adopt this one if you like, observe its comings and goings. You may learn a lot from it because, you see, it has no fear.

That is the key.

6

Here come the children, a little ahead of themselves, shouting and throwing streamers of laughter. They roll and they tumble. If they have a ball, they roll and tumble that. If they have a dog, they do the same. It's all hugely messy. No point in making a fuss. There'll be time for nostalgia later, along with the cleaning up.

The children are laughing in many colours. They fall apart laughing, and come together laughing. They laugh on one foot. Then the other. They laugh as they hop back and forth. They do a handstand and laugh upside down. They laugh on the upswing and on the downswing. They throw laughter around like balls of paint, splashing it everywhere, all over the grass and the graves and the picnic basket. Rag ends of merriment get smudged on the sky.

Nothing terrifies them. They are careless of life, and death has a way of evading them. For a time they are laughing, at least.

They are playing hopscotch. To play hop-scotch, eight squares are laid out like little graves, and the children must hop from one to the other. On one foot, then the other, then both. Over the graves they hop. *Hop, turn, jump, laugh.*

I asked my parents for 15 cents,
To see the platypus jump the fence.
She jumped so high she touched the sky,
And didn't come back till the Fourth of July.

One, two, three, how many children can you see? They keep scores and accuse each other of cheating, then forget about all that. When the picnic basket is open, they leapfrog right in. One after the other... *one, two, three.*

I asked my parents for 15 cents,
To see the platypus jump the fence.

I am laughing and you are sombre. This is all very new to you, I know, here at the edge of the world, but I have to grab every opportunity to seize the day. You know the old rhyme as well as I do:

In the moment of our talking, envious time has ebb'd away.

Seize the present; trust tomorrow even as little as you may.

The children are laughing because the sky and earth are making such a racket doing what everything else is doing. A hurricane of sighs and a whirlpool of whispers. *Do this and I will love you forever. Do that and I will love you even longer.*

Tear me apart

and I will put you back together

set me up

and knock me over like a feather.

Whispering whirlpools. The children will laugh behind their hands, and make rude gestures, because the dish has run away with the spoon, and there is nothing anybody can do about it, no matter how hard they try.

The child who wins the hopscotch is the one who can stay in the air the longest.

You can still hear the shouts long after feet have hit the ground.

Their voices float on the wind, but nobody hears them.

7

If I talk about myself in the third person, it's out of necessity. I've never been comfortable as a first person. It seems a bit grandiose. It's been a very long time since I've been any kind of person, although I do have some memories that belong to someone. Of course there are memories lying about all over the place here; it's easy enough to trip over them unawares.

I am taking a buggy ride down a long tree-lined avenue. I must be lying on my back, like a baby, because I can see trees passing each side of me, as if we are sliding down a long tunnel. I'm sure I played hopscotch with the children and jumped from grave to grave, from life to life, my feet just briefly touching the ground. I can see the laughter, like falling stars streaking the sky.

Memories or dreams – call them what you will, they are coiled up inside me with the birth and the death of suns and the great falling apart of matter and energy. This material of which I am made, this physical body, comes from stones and rock and earth, but my voice was born in the star fires. If I was human, it was only very briefly. I sat upon the road with my hand out. I worshipped whatever gods were on offer, and got whipped for it. I put myself above others and got pulled down for it. That's about the extent of my human occupation. You can't ask much more of me in that respect.

Here I am, nothing more than an arc of stone. Like you, I am composed of fragments of the cosmos. Just a humble headstone sitting in a secluded corner of a minor galaxy.

There it sits. Really, it has no 'me'.

It only exists in this moment because you are seeing it.

The only question is, what's written there?

8

Whatever the appearances, a headstone has no beliefs.

Take me, for example. You might have noticed the concrete angel with mossy wings, or the dove in cement lace, that perch upon my arc of stone, and roost there between flights to the neverworld.

They are not works of art, more approximations of an idea the stonemaker had. A stumbling attempt at metaphor.

A headstone cannot afford beliefs, because it is where beliefs come to die or wear away over time. Beliefs are like memories, they are effaced or defaced or retraced in the swinging about of the sun. Soon they are no longer recognisable. Moss obliterates the concrete angel into one messy lump; the dove sleeps in a song. You may believe in them if you wish. Believe in what you think they represent. Worship that which offers itself up in good faith if you must.

I must remain silent on these matters. I've seen too many faiths come to grief, too many gods made to kneel. Everywhere I look old Ozymandias is still exhorting his subjects to look upon his works and despair.

Trying to sort out all that is beyond the province of a humble headstone made of nothing more than rock and shadow.

Does it matter to the stone what is scratched on its surface?

9

Here comes the girl with the skipping rope. She's an occasional visitor and not a part of the hopscotch gang. Note how aloof she is from the other children. She has come from the street, from the school of hard knocks, and I wonder sometimes if she is a child at all. She seems so independent. Nothing seems to faze her.

You can call her the skipping girl. Under her flying rope the years skip by.

You'd think she was a welcome diversion from all of this, but she knows the score. She's not easily fooled. She often appears out of nowhere; that's her style. She is accountable to no one. In this case hers is a courtesy visit only. Her hop, skip and jump propels her through the many worlds. Three worlds in as many instants – *hop skip jump*. Three in one go!

She skips between the rows of fairy tales right up the witch's door. That would be Baba Yaga of the Iron Teeth. If you've never heard of her, you have now. I'm sorry about that because becoming aware of her is not a pleasant experience. It's like waking up to the sense that there is somebody else in the room. She likes to be spooky. She is not someone you would want to run into on a dark night, or visit with a fistful of flowers. Those iron teeth were made for crunching up children. She can chomp up children bones and all.

Supremely indifferent, the skipping girl skips around the witch's hut, the one that can run around on chicken legs, while

Baba Yaga watches helplessly from inside. It's a consummate cameo performance. When it's done the skipping girl skips off back down the rows of headstones where all the fairy tales are buried.

She seems so blithe and fancy free it's too easy to envy her. She can skip from world to world, story to story, joy to joy, while we are stuck here in my shadow under one eternal sky.

It takes a bit of getting used to, I know. You came here quite innocently, clutching a posy of flowers you bought from the flower-seller at the gate. She was a poor young woman with nothing else to sell. You thought you might donate your posy to some needy headstone, and quite casually happened by me.

You weren't looking for any of this, I understand. Especially not the sudden pain of envy, the heartburn of regret, the impossibility of sandcastle memories. At one time you too vaulted through worlds. Then you forgot. Now you suffer the agony of remembering, remembering how you could float through the air like a puff of dandelion and brush the sky with a feather.

Ha ha, be patient. The skipping girl has that kind of effect on people. I've seen grown men and women break down and cry just watching her. Her rope whizzes right through their heads on its long, elliptical orbit. All kinds of grief gets stirred up. Somebody remembers; somebody forgets; somebody makes a pass at somebody; somebody passes out under a rose bush. Somebody dies of love, somebody dies of loneliness. Somebody else just dies. It's all a wild rumpus.

Whizz whizz whizz, goes her rope. Suns and moons and

cosmic dust fly everywhere.

There is nothing new under the sun or in the shadow of the headstone. You may see such a girl. You may see fireflies at night pop and fizzle too. It's no use envying her. There's no time for folderol. Envy or jealously or martyrdom or whatever it is you are feeling have no place beneath the wings of the concrete angel.

The skipping girl has skipped right out of any story you might start to build for her.

Stories are so temping, aren't they? But she is up and around the bend, out of sight already. She doesn't belong in your story, or anybody else's. She's returned to the street. There's no time, even for an aftertaste, as Baba Yaga is aroused now. Her hut has got up on its chicken legs. It's you she's after. Children are a nice entree, if you can catch them, but let's consider the main course!

You didn't think of that, did you, when you followed the skipping girl up the garden path?

10

There are limitations, although these are hard to see at first. You may flee, but only from one side of the headstone to the other. That's a huge distance when you come to actually traverse it, in real time. It's an ecstatic distance. It can hardly be crossed in calm and quiet although we love these things. It may take a moment or a lifetime, there's no telling. There's no booking in advance.

You may sing, but only for as long as a tuning fork holds its note.

There's not much time for anything but a necessary singing, even in flight. Weeping gets left behind with the weepers; fear gets left behind with the fearful; dreams get left behind with the sleepers; mountains get left behind in the ocean. Distances are measured in song. Movements are measured in feeling.

But only as long as the tuning fork holds it note.

Everything is in the wind. It was from the start, the first rapturous point of origin. The very first skip. The first whizz of the rope. The first beat of a mineral heart. The first rainbow of syllables that set time in action.

Baba Yaga was there right at the beginning too. You just didn't see her until the skipping girl came along with her magic rope, unfolding fairy tales in all directions, but she was there nevertheless, thinking up recipes for cooking children.

You can run, but you cannot know where your feet will land.

You can turn your head but you don't know what your eyes will see.

The spider always slings her web across the most fanciful spaces.

11

This is rather difficult for both of us, finding common ground here in the three dimensional world of life, birth and death. It is true that you are never far away from the sound of a baby crying or the ululation of mourners. Or the quick breaths between.

I can offer no more than a momentary respite from all the whoosh and hurtle of life; shadows move on, even for a headstone. But it's no use turning to me as if I were responsible. You turn to me when there is nowhere else to turn. That makes more sense. I wouldn't be anybody's first option.

You need to understand that I don't have any investment in this. There's nothing hanging on the outcome. People come and go. Some of them leave flowers. Some of them leave nothing. Some of them don't leave at all. Most last as long as the tuning fork holds its note, the time it takes the song to go from one side of the headstone to another.

Everything is haunted by eternity. Even the sharp bark of dog or the distant cry of a gull. Nothing gets away scot-free.

Nor am I a public service. I'm not a railway station or a bank. I'm not a drinking fountain or object d'art. I'm not a juke-box or an information terminal. There are so many things I'm not; it would take a lifetime to list them.

This is not a court of appeal, or a theme park, or a public execution, or just a place to bring the kids for a picnic. Despite appearances, memories don't last long around here. Gulls are always on the lookout for leftovers. This the place of perpetual shedding, a constant scraping away. Don't be fooled by spiders and cockroaches. One appearance follows another until an outline becomes visible. A horizon line, a shape, a movement. Eventually the figure of a headstone shaped like a tuning fork. What could be more resonant? More designer made for the purpose? Take it off. Scrape it all off! The moss and the meaning, the dead skin of the world. Let the wind turn you. Bend to the four directions.

Step from the shadow to the stage. If it is a place of perpetual shedding, it is also a place of heartache. A place to bare yourself to your tormentor, at long last. A place where the choices are few and the consequences immediate. You'll get the hang of it, like walking without supports after a long convalescence. It doesn't have to be humiliating, unless you want it that way.

For some, humiliation is a timely reminder. I'm not in a position to make any judgements.

If you have come to me for judgement you have come to the wrong place. That's not my department. That's down the hall and up the garden path.

12

What I am is a simple headstone, with a mossy angel on top. An angel with abnegating wings. And a dove in cement lace, still asleep inside a song. These are afterthoughts, haphazardly executed. They look silly, decorating the otherwise clean curvature of stone.

None of this is particularly reassuring. You look around for the clothes you shed but some trickster has run off them. Now your electric skin is turning to goosebumps. Yesterday has become impossible; tomorrow is another graveyard. Already there are too many dead. You bump into them everywhere, the thankless dead. You'd wonder why they bother, what business they can have here, but I would ask you the same thing. You can't hold out forever. Sooner or later they shut the gates and snip the padlocks. That keeps everybody out but the lovers who like to lie down with the dead, and a few drunks who climb over their lives and get lost among the headstones.

We have a regular who does that. He drinks and becomes nostalgic for the grave. He dreams of vast, wide open spaces, plains and uplands. He dreams of yellow tussock and an ocean the colour of iron. He dreams of leapfrogging over foothills to the sounds of chanting children. *What's the time Mr Wolfie...?* When he wakes it is with a sense of overwhelming shame and exhaustion. And the only cure for that is the day's first drink.

You didn't ask for any of this, I know. You wandered in quite casually, bearing flowers, not quite sure what you were seeking. Maybe you were looking for a little grief, a little solitude, freedom from the dues ex machina that always looms large in your narrative. The cavalry are coming. The cavalry are always coming. The cavalry are still coming. Grief is never far away from the laughter of children. Perhaps for a moment you thought of yourself as a mourner. You joined the procession, not to mourn this life or that, but out of a more general sympathy for all mourners.

Judgement is very far away. The figure by your side is very near. You look to me for guidance of some kind. But I'm not a map or a territory. I'm not a Lonely Planet travel guidebook, and I don't give directions to tourists. If you look at me hard enough you might read something there. A word or two. A date. If you're lucky, a pious sentiment – *And flights of angels sing thee to thy rest.* Or more simply, *Into the sunshine.* Or, *Speak your love still once again.* Or how about, *He broke through the barriers of the skies.*

Green my heart green
Blue it blue
Song it for the dolphins and the children.
Language is never at rest.

Some come here to make amends; some come to learn to fly. Still others are just tired.

No point in bleeding too hard.

13

It is starting to occur to you that this is not what it appears to be. You came with flowers to bear witness to this day, to this moment, to this juncture. These minutes passing, the needle sliding. The flowers bore witness; you were struck blind. In your mind, the gates are always open, never padlocked shut. There's always a way back, through the gate, through the streets, through the filth and the dirty air, to the places you remember just around the corner of mind, where the light is gentle and women call to each other across comfortable spaces. You can taste the olives and feta and crispy rocket. Hear the Gregorian chant of sunrises.

You do not leave as a mourner, or picnicker, or child. You do not leave at all. You were never a mourner. You arrival was not accidental; it never is. People come in search of me. That makes no sense, I know, but there you have it. There's no accounting for the winds that blow. In all the places in all the worlds, this is perhaps the least of them. There is no Taj Mahal in the shadow of the headstone, merely a word or two.

You didn't picnic on the grass. You didn't play hopscotch with the children. I doubt that you ever saw the skipping girl. Now that it's time for everybody to go back to their lives, you are in a quandary. You have many lives, none of them you can go back to, not with any peace of mind. When you look at those lives, none of them are what they're cracked up to be. Nothing to write home about. All kinds of hints and misdirection, false starts and misplaced hopes. One life blurs into another until none of them have any substance.

The headstone is the size of the world or the size of a handkerchief, depending on your point of view. The cockroach and the crow have little in common, but their lives are bound together in Faraway. The wind shakes the web.

We are not the mourners but the mourned.

14

Consider those around you. All they have ever asked for is truth and plain speaking, and all they have received are lies and riddles. Around and around goes the skipping rope, *whoosh whoosh.*

Ask no questions and you'll be told no lies

Keep your trap shut and you'll catch no flies

Complicated things are made simple and simple things are made complicated; in this way the living are kept in a state of maximum confusion. The barbarians are always at the gate, always on the point of making a grand entry. The keepers of the kingdom wear blindfolds. The asphodels keep their faith. The cypress strives upward. Spectres drift through the blood and the dust. The war never ended. Privilege never dies on the battlefield.

You are faced with a few home truths, which is never a pleasant experience. One day the headstone will crack open like a mourner's heart. A million words will spill out but to no avail. These words are like fireflies, they light up the night, but I'm not sure that they can crawl through holes in the world the way the cockroach can. I'm not sure they can burrow through time or survive the singularity of a black hole.

The headstone will split and its edges will crumble away. You can see that one coming, I'm sure. Everyday erosion is enough to do the trick, no special effects required. Eventually, even stone will melt back into the air. Words will return to their texts. The dead will click their tickets and make a run for the hell-bound train.

It's all in the dreams of moss and the rust of iron. The cement angel might last a little longer, its wings folded deep into the stone. You can hold it in the palm of your hand. You can breathe on it. You can throw it into the air and close your eyes. It might be buoyed in the air by the laughter of the children. Or it might break apart when it hits the sun.

15

I will suffer the same desolation as the rest of the cosmos, even if these words do create their own singularity. Gravity's fighting a losing battle. You can watch all the other headstones speeding away from us at rapidly increasing velocities; gravity is helpless in face that that outward thrust. Soon we will be alone, you and I. A brisk wind blows a candy wrapper across grass. The same wind shreds voices that tend to linger in courtyards and coffee shops along with the sights and smells.

Our consciousness is required to sustain this great separation, the falling apart of matter and energy, then the falling apart of matter from matter, energy from energy, until the last quantum of heat dissipates into the cold clay.

I will be gone and you will be a memory. Everybody who comes here, even by accident, ends up wondering why parts of themselves are starting to recede.

These are the rag ends of days. I think you know them, or at least you've heard of them. Things that are buried rise again. Contrary winds blow. I think you know why you're here and what you're doing in the shadow of the headstone. It's not that hard to work out. Eventually, the penny drops. You didn't have to worm through a hole in the world to get here, or crawl across the curve of space. You wandered, perhaps unwittingly, across the drift of streets, and now just find yourself here, at the same time understanding that there is nowhere else to be. This is the moment, here in the shadow of the headstone, where time, place and memory conjoin for the briefest moment of apprehension.

Whatever way it happens, even the headstone has to confront its own crumbling edges. I bear witness for as long as the names and the dates and the fine sentiments stay etched on stone. For that time and no longer. I can hold the memory, but only for as long as the stone lasts. Eventually it must succumb to the mists of early dawn wherein history is buried. Eventually it must dissipate like a puff of smoke from the addict's pipe. It can only last as long as the bonds of gravity allow. It's all very solemn, and full of pious remembrance, until somebody giggles and gives the game away. In one short, barking laugh the stone breaks open. The name is split in two.

Don't walk on the grass.

16

As one person remembers, another forgets. Your loss is my loss. A monkey has climbed over the headstone to get in. The whole place is crawling with ants and tears. The ants are having a picnic. The tears are looking for a convenient rock to hide under. The last franchise pulls down the sky and replaces it with another one, one that smiles. The sky is an asterisk. The picnickers pack up their troubles in their old kit bags. A floppy dog gets called to heel. A few words are left behind for the gulls. Powered by the force of creation, the fragments all speed away from one another like stars in the ever-expanding universe, like the dreams of a headstone.

There's an even-handedness in all this that is easy to overlook. Remembering and forgetting, losing and winning, picking up and putting down, bending over and straightening up, digging graves and filling them in – the list is endless. Every action has its equal and opposite reaction. Consciousness is reciprocal. After a while it's easy enough to feel trapped. If it's not one thing it's another. There's no way out that isn't back in. There is no sky that isn't a mirror, no word without a shadow. There is no wisdom that can't be turned upside down. No wave without a particle. No zig without a zag. It is very easy to feel trapped, desperate even, being caught in the ebb and the flow. Drowned or left high and dry. No rest for the wicked, as they say. Or anybody else for that matter.

There's an even-handedness to living and dying also, or

have you forgotten that in your haste to get somewhere? Since energy cannot be created or destroyed, you were never born and will never die. The kiss of death becomes the breath of life.

At the same time, every moment of your existence will be matched by a moment of non-existence. Within the headstone, these two things become one thing. The opposites become apposite. The children hold hands and dance in a circle. First one way, then the other. Words do the same. First one way, then the other. Forwards and backwards. One person cries out; the world answers. Another person cries out; everybody keeps mum.

You lie down in your grave but you can't die. You sit up in your grave but you can't climb out of the headstone. All that even-handedness you are just starting to understand.

17

If you look at it objectively, you didn't arrive at the gate with much. The clutch of flowers don't count, the handful of hopes the same. In any game, everything depends on what you can put on the table. Not much use sitting down to play with empty pockets.

So what have you got?

An old clock that's lost its tick.

A couple of faded photographs.

Some papier-mâché faces with no eyebrows.

Some foreign coins.

A begging bowl of memories.

A street that got lost on the way home.

A door with a broken handle.

A valuable nail.

A flower-seller with a pretty smile.

Now that you come to look at it, there's not much on offer. People are always amazed that after a lifetime of accumulation, they arrive at the gate with so little. A few things flung clear. Mostly just fragments of imagination in the Catherine Wheel sky.

When you remember people, you remember ships that pass in the night heading for their own dark shores. You remember treats at the picnic, and chocolate smiles. Everybody was saved or died laughing. You couldn't understand half of it; the language was hard to learn. All around you people spoke of incomprehensible things, made gestures with their hands and expected you to do the same.

Everybody rides off into the sunset, taking the illusion with them. And if they can't ride, they walk. There's not much left over for you, just a few curled sandwiches and raisin pies, but that's all right because it was never much different. It was always changing into something else. Consider your own case. You were raised on the smell of an oily rag. You spent all those years in the belly of a whale. Then you went into the desert to draw a line in the sand somewhere. All that took a while. When you returned, the world had changed. The river you used to fish had dried up.

You turn up here with no more collateral than a few words in a blindfold.

I'm sure you can do better than that.

18

It's too easy to feel put on the spot, singled out for special treatment, but I am not accusing you of anything. Everybody is implicated every time they draw breath. And me, I don't stand aside as comfortably as you might think. I have memories too, I have scraps to arrange, flowers to bury. I can sit here like an infant playing with my food, moving it around, and forget all about being a simple headstone in some minor corner of a minor galaxy.

I've got all sorts of things to deal with. After all, it's been quite a picnic. The usual chaos.

The little dog laughed
to see such craft,
and the dish ran away with the spoon.

Meanwhile the hard-boiled egg, still half inside its shell, practices its dialogue with a piece of toast. A cut of lamb floats to the top of the alphabet soup.

All the time there are bones to look after, the same grave announcement to make to the world. It's not all beer and skittles being a headstone. All that remains is a scraping of letters, crumbled stone and moss, and the far off melodies of nursery rhymes.

All those rocking horse dreams. I don't know what to do with them any more than you do. They seem to offer marvels, but I don't see any. Just the same old same old. People don't come here for the view.

19

It's harder to pin the world down than people think. Just when they think they have a handle on things, the handle flies off. Just when they think they have found the word, the word missteps. Just when they get a grip, the grip slips. There's a quantum slipperiness to ordinary things people factor out, because we can't live, at least not yet, within that kind of complexity.

So we smooth it over, smooth down the lumps, doctor the evidence, straighten the curve, try to unstep the misstep. But they are only temporary expedients. At some point it breaks down. Things go lumpy again. The evidence jumps up and hits you in the face.

It happens to everybody, if they let it. Then it happens whether they let it or not. Take you own case. We think we know why you're here, but there it is – you walk through a gate, and nothing is the same again. You buy some flowers from the flower seller and carry her smile with you along the paths between the headstones.

You stand in front of a random headstone so that everybody will think that you are someone else, and the headstone turns out to be not quite so random after all, even if you can't quite read the name.

All around us people are talking or staying silent. Everybody has a different tale to tell, and nobody is admitting too much. There are histories written and histories that are never written. It all depends on your point of view, whether you are the sparrow or the word. As one person remembers, another forgets. One person puts down the sword, another picks it up. Somebody writes a word, another finds it. Someone pauses to buy flowers and watch the children playing hopscotch. The same happens with words. You can smooth them down, but they will go lumpy on you at a moment's notice.

There's a big mish-mash of coming and going. Galaxies appear and disappear at the speed of light. Words do the same. You can see, but you can't comprehend. Your monkey brain will never escape the headstone. Your words will never catch up with the world. Even fragments don't last long enough for you to get a handle on them. They quickly dissolve and recombine into other things, skies and seas and all the cities of the headstone. Blood and rust; blossom and rain.

20

The words that are engraved upon me are not necessarily easy to decipher. The same moss that covers the angel with abnegating wings, eats into the headstone, and softly blurs the chiselled lettering. To read these words you have to be blind. It's easier that way. You have to grope with your hands. It's unseemly, but it gets the job done.

After a while, however, you're not sure they are your hands any more. You feel for the name with fingers already numb but find moss and crumbled stone where once there were shapes. Each letter becomes a puzzle, an enigma, a secret sign, a star that falls from the mouth of god. Is that an E or an F? Is that a C or an O? How far can your finger trace this glyph before the trail peters out in the rough stone, the curvature of space?

What is harder is the terror these questions generate, the instability. Our hopes and fears now count for nothing. The word, whatever it is, might remain forever beyond your grasp, or rather your feel. Your fingers will give out before the world reveals its secrets. The song will give out before you can hear it. The door will close before it disappears.

And yet you can't let it go. It holds some terrific significance, that special word, if only you could find it. Time and place; place and time. It must still be there in the layers of memory, like a steel trap under autumn leaves. Once you have worked through the quantum uncertainties, collapsed all the probability fronts and finally found it, you can spring it and call it your own. You can tame it to the headstone. Chisel it deeper this time, pound the blade home into the stone. Tattoo the word with a jackhammer. Make the chips fly. Spread yourself across the S-matrix like a bird spreads its wings.

It's no use trying to trace the epitaph on paper, or fool the world with plastic flowers. The world always remains one step ahead; it is never at rest. You can't quite catch up. You can't get to the end of the headstone. Join the queue! There's a long line of refugees stretching around the corner. Each carries a word, sacred to themselves.

All this suffering has to do with truth, but even the truth, when you find it with your broken hands – *In Loving Memory Of* – even that becomes a lie after a time. The truth that serves some purpose other than truth itself becomes a lie. The common phrases, the trite and the polite – *I am very sorry for your loss. Their sacrifices will never be forgotten.* Never is a big word. You can't carve remembrance into the never-never, and eventually everybody dies or forgets how to read. The headstone collects them all in. I am always at hand. There are no exceptions. The names are legion. A generation passes and nobody remembers except the stone, which remembers in name only.

You might as well carve your words on air.

21

Stay awhile, and you start to see things from my point of view. To do that you have to put metaphysics away and sit down with me. See the world through the headstone. Let the vertical gently give way to the horizontal. Let the parallel lines soften in the distance. Let's draw the field of vision closer. Let's be like the child who pulls the horizon up under their chin and hopes for the best.

I get a beggar's eye view of the world, but there's not much to see. It's a pretty minimal landscape: *keep off the grass.* Even a beggar is rich in the passing parade of legs, the long and short and the tall. Beggars may choose the busiest places; headstones don't have that luxury. Not much hustle and bustle around here, although the picnic looks like a lot of fun. Everybody is filling their faces, kids screaming, dogs barking, blood flowing. The living and the dead meet here in no-man's-land. They shake hands. They swap jokes, they play hopscotch, they share their rations from the picnic basket. Suddenly war is very far away; Jupiter is very close. There's a crescent moon waiting in the wings to crown the morning star.

Here comes a woman in a drab brown coat and old-fashioned stockings with seams. And doeskin gloves with seams. She's probably looking for the skipping girl who she follows around. But she always comes up and greets me as if I were an old friend. She never brings flowers, she's not the flower bringing type, but she has this one curious gesture – she reaches out and caresses the stone angel with the abnegating wings. There's a tenderness in it that always takes me by surprise.

It's a brief enough movement, and she doesn't say anything, but I am invariably moved by it. A small enough gesture from the repertoire of grief, doeskin fingers on corroding stone. A light but lingering blessing.

Sit with me long enough, share my beggar's eye view of the world for long enough, and you begin to see around the edges of the air, around the corners of words. It's all done with mirrors and pullies. You can't be fooled by the apparent transparency of words any more than by the blueness of the sky. Or the wisdom of the headstone, being as thick as a brick. There's all sorts of other stuff going on outside the headlights, the field of vision. A hectic world full of things. Things that go clang and bang, day or night.

Out of the corner of your eye you can glimpse the figure that stands beside you. This figure throws a shadow, and that shadow is you, the one who peers out, blinking at the world. That's why it's so hard to get focus on this mysterious shape. These things depend on a slip of the eye, a slip of the word. Perhaps all this is nothing more than concussion. *What's the time Mr Wolfie?*

It takes a moment for you to realize that this companion of yours isn't going away. The dog that peed on the headstone, the skipping girl who bravely skipped right up to Baba Yaga's door, even the picnickers – they have all gone away. That has sort of narrowed down the field. It's harder not to see the form standing beside you. A slip of the mind. It knows things you should know. It brings you back to the headstone. It reminds you of your life. That figure has always been with you, a silent attendant. It was the first thing you saw after opening your eyes to the world. It is the first thing you remember when you close your eyes to the world.

Perhaps to see it properly you have to see it from my beggar's eye view of the world. I get to see things most people don't notice. I get to see the world upside-down and sideways. I get to turn the world around and see it from the other side. I get to shake it around to see what words fall out.

22

You were there at the beginning, is it possible that you won't be there at the end, that you will sit this one out? I doubt it. The figure by your side doubts it. It's double or nothing. His double; your double. Then it's all or nothing. Then it's nothing at all. The big cancellation. That's how a life goes. You can't sit it out. While the music plays, you stay on your feet.

The figure beside you will always dance should you choose to turn in that direction. Yes, you have heard this music before. When it stops, everybody will scramble for their graves. There won't be enough graves to go around, that's for sure. There'll be a lot of restless spirits hunting for their headstones.

...and the little dog laughed to see such craft...

You can't cop out, that's the bitch of it. The day cuts deep or not at all. You either stay in bed or get up; the choice is stark. You can't throw in the towel and swallow your losses along with the champagne because you are already bleeding, already one of the walking wounded. Everybody's on borrowed time. You always thought cowardice was an option, a last resort. You could always slip out the back door. At the end of the day, cowardice would get you through, you thought. Every dog has its day, then turns tail and runs. Now, in the shadow of the headstone, escape doesn't seem so likely. There is no back door.

Whichever way you turn, you are always facing the headstone. The four directions have turned into one, and your feet are planted there. There is no reprieve. All kinds of options are closing down. Doors are shutting in your face and turning into walls. The sound of gunfire is never far away, like doors shutting on the horizon. *Slam, slam, slam* – a hard wind blows. The house of cards gets the shakes. Cowards die too, friend, just like the brave. Easy to die in a hard wind in a house of tenderness with the Jack and the Queen. You just have to lean out a little too far from the flimsy streets. You can wait it out – or grab a gun.

That sound is getting closer, don't you think? One slam after the other. Here a roof gone; here a wall; here a window with a glass map. The house cannot stand. Nations go the same way. From riches to rubble. Everyone has a relative to bury.

No use huddling in the shadow of the headstone. I can't protect you. All I can do is know where the shadow will fall.

23

It always comes this way, like a thief in the night, this figure beside you, this other you whose mere shadow you are. How does it come to be that it's you who are its pale reflection? Shouldn't it be the other way around? you are asking. After all, it is here, on the path, before the headstone, where you standing, that is the real world. The world where the picnic is spread and the children play hopscotch and *the little dog laughed to see such craft...*

The duplicity of this figure mirrors your own. You've hardly arrived, but already you are planning your escape, cash in your Get Out of Dodge Free card and skip the twilight. Do you think that will work? Do you think the dead won't know you, that they won't recognise you on the street during some ordinary day, or at night when the owls gather at your window? That figure, standing by your side is blindfolded, blindsided, mutilated – knows you only too well. Sees right through you in fact.

This is your real self, telling you what to do in this exigency: Put on the blindfold. Listen for footsteps in the dark. Read the signs. Make your peace with the grave. Bind your hands within the headstone as you would in supplication. The laughter of children, just around the corner for you. The sorrows of motherhood sit on the other side of god. The laughter of children fades in the twilight.

You aim to find all those left-over words you didn't find at the party, after the lolly scramble. There are lots of words, but they're not coming to the rescue. They're hiding in all sorts of unlikely places, every nook and cranny. You'll also find bits and pieces that don't fit anywhere else, like the man reading a newspaper on a park bench. He looks like he wandered in here by mistake. And the lovers who couldn't face the head-stone without holding hands, and who couldn't move without treading on their tears. And the dead soldiers who passed into history, taking their stories and headstones with them – a wave of pride and knives.

These are just the scraps of history, more than you can shake a stick at.

When the figure standing by your side moves, you move, and I move too. It all depends on your point of view. You have to move. You have to change with the changing configuration that you sparked. As you move, everything moves around you. The shadows shift around according to your perspective. And everything around them shifts according to their angle on life. There is no point of view that isn't shifting around some other shifting point of view.

As far as I can see, there is no omniscient point of view unless it is buried deep in the headstone, beyond the reach of any code. You can't trust the shadows to stay in one place, why would you want to? You can't trust your point of view to stay in one place either, how could it, with you at such sixes and sevens?

And yet... there is a certain reciprocity in it. When you rise to your feet, the world rises with you. When you come to an understanding, your shadow meets you half-way. When you pretend it's not there, it pretends you're not there and you start to feel unloved. Unloved and unwanted.

And now the day goes on without you. You can no longer

bring the self into a relation of fit to the external world.

The thief in the night has stolen the moon.

24

Within the compass of the headstone, all things are possible. You might be asleep or dead or just marking time, but all things that can happen will happen and have probably already happened. That's why you keep seeing the same images again and again, in different configurations. That's why you begin to feel that there's no way out, that everywhere you turn the vista is the same. You begin to suspect that the front and the back of the headstone are one and the same thing.

The things that went away come swirling back. They have a different life now. Whatever they once were is lost to gravitational shift. The woman in the shabby brown coat seems to have wandered through the gate from another story, while the gloved hand on the concrete angel comes from even further back and from another city entirely. The dog with the floppy ears hangs around to pee a second time before being shooed away by the kids playing hopscotch. The skipping girl skips right back in and makes up a new story, one in which she is the heroine. She vanquishes Baba Yaga, cooks her up in a big stew for the picnic, and sells her iron teeth at the flea market, where they become a part of someone else's story. *Those iron teeth you have strung into a necklace, they look so realistic...*

In that story, or some other, the picnickers invite you to their feast, and you pull up a piece of sky – you do remember that – and sit down with them. Have a glass of wine. Shoo away the dog. Play hopscotch with the children. You learn all over again to jump on one foot, then the other, then both feet. And spin around in midair at the same time. Fun and games! *What's the time Mr Woolfie?*

We've heard that mocking chant before somewhere, haven't we? We can share a moment with that one. The echo comes from way back. It's bounced through many hills and streets to get here, to find a resting place, as it were. There are so many worlds. Spin in midair and land on a different one each time. The music of the spheres is rich. You can't live in them all. You don't have that many lifetimes – at least not here.

We don't have to worry about mortality, you know. People have all the lifetimes in the world, as long as it takes. Certainly the headstone doesn't care. I am just a medium in which these things can exist. In fact, I know nothing of them. The profound indifference of the headstone disturbs you; its silly homilies annoy you. *Rest in peace*! Ha ha. Your perceptual field has narrowed down. The figure by your side has taken everything you can see, bit by bit, and consigned it to the headstone, like someone feeding wood into a fire. Everything is consumed. All the juice and joy, all the lives it was possible to live.

And when the figure by your side touches you with its gloved hand, you will fold your cement wings back into the headstone. There is the miracle of your world, and the miracle of you seeing it. This world is held in place by the power of revelation alone. That tiny kink in spacetime that is you will soon be smoothed over. A crackle in your ears and it will all be over. Death can't hold it all together; it's too big a job for a little thing like death.

The gloved hand will return to memory.

Where the picnic blanket spread, the grass lies flat.

25

I know how confusing this must all be for you. You thought you were getting somewhere. Making progress. Getting there. You came here to mourn, not to die to the world; to visit the headstone, not move in with it. You felt the crunch of gravel under your feet, smelled the fragrances of the day, heard the chant of children, tasted food from the picnic, and sobbed into your handkerchief. Doubts were very far away. You had a story all ready, one you'd brought with you. A narrative with all the bobs and whistles. It was made to fit. To fit you. Your story anchored you in the world. Above all, it was a true story, that was its great strength. You could tell it to anybody with perfect confidence, pretty much. It got you out of all kinds of tricky situations. The truth brightens any day. You could pass through the wrought-iron gates with a nod, and smile at the prospect of children paying hopscotch on the grass. You could breathe in the air and breathe out the sky knowing they would still be there afterwards. You could touch the light with your warm hands without turning a hair. It wasn't that complicated. It was just being alive. Not too many words. Only enough to outfit thought, no more no less. Enough focused attention to bring the self into a relation of fit to the external world. Enough for you to feel the congruence of the word to the world. Enough for you to feel pretty happy with yourself.

26

There's a touch of panic when you realize that all that you once held in your mortal hands is now unreachable. The material world looks more like smoke on the water.

This is not what you bargained for. People wander about, in and out of their lives, looking for this or that. Is it under the chair? Is it behind the sofa? Has it taken refuge in a drawer somewhere? What was it I wanted in the first place? You're not one of those fools. You're something else. You don't deserve to be ripped away from the world, or worse, deceived away from it by all these slippery words that run on and on and blur all necessary boundaries. When it's time to leave, you can't get away from them. They cling to you like burrs on wool. They make nonsense of a world that makes perfect sense, turning order and certainty into an alphabet soup, turning neatly laid paths and trimmed lawns.

Or perhaps you are one of those fools, rolling every likely

looking rock looking for their lives, leaving no stone unturned, gambling on all kinds of unlikely odds. You approach me like a journeyman or supplicant. The headstone has become the entrance to a cave in which resides the fabled Keeper of Secrets. The skipping girl is her apprentice. You have been here before although you won't admit it to yourself. That was back in the day. Lots of water under the bridge, lots of blood on the sheets. A picnic in a park. A fragrance and a fading song. There is so much that has to remain secret, even to you, even to me, because it has not yet been revealed. It has not yet been declared. Nothing has been approved. No pattern has appeared. It will happen in the fullness of time, they say. All will be revealed. All will be made clear. The name is there, loud and clear, even if you no longer have the fingers to read it.

27

Although everything has changed, you want nothing to change. The more things change the more they stay the same, you like to say. It sounds comforting. That's everybody's story. Yet change is the only god visible to the human eye. All the rest is speculation. Change gives and change takes away. The rest is tenderness.

All we want to do is continue on as before, business as usual. We pay lip service to change and carry on regardless. You are not immune. Expect the unexpected, you say, and yet you still expect the grass to grow, the rain to come and the debts to get paid. You expect to hold the earth beneath your feet without getting mud between your toes. You expect the air to fit your hands like a candy wrapper. You expect the picnickers to arrive at any moment, bringing the world with them. You expect the flowers to wilt on time. You expect the headstone to colour the clouds in a mourner's grey. You expect the spider to climb up into the sky and reclaim all the world's stories. You expect the joyous laughter of children. All these expectations; all that sacrifice! The plotting and planning. The betting on outcomes. The pulling of monkey faces at the clock.

So much has been promised, it seems.

Promises are thick on the ground before the sun rises; it's easy, even necessary, to make promises in the dark.

But a promise is not made of stone, like I am, crumbling or not. Look hard and there's just moss and lies and neglected spiderwebs. If there's a word in there, nobody's noticed. When you touch the headstone with your gloved fingers, they come away smudged with moss. That's the first step. You want to make a joke about the rolling stone but the joke gathers no moss. You can't play this one for the laughs. You can't even go back to the picnic and the promise of the picnic basket.

Moss spreads from your fingers to your arms. That's not a promise, it's an infection. It's not inspiration, it's an illness. You drown the promises, along with your blithe assumptions, as you would drown a bagful of cats. With difficulty.

Looking back, we struggle to make sense of our lives. We

are never far from mythology. You tried to find the name on the headstone and bruised your fingers, and that's when everything turned pear-shaped, when the hour-glass turned over.

That's a story of a kind too, a shape-shifting moment. The problem with that story is that you're still there, still here, by the headstone, your fingers scratching at the mossy letters. Nothing has happened but a little blood on the headstone. No time has passed. The sun has paused in the sky. A child has paused in mid-shout. The skipping girl has frozen in the air, her hair flying.

The story is on pause, mid-word.

28

It's true that nothing turns out the way you thought. Not even memory. Memory holds out a few promises – for a while. Memories seem to offer pleasant relief from the arrow of time. You can put your feet up and take a well-earned break. Forget for a moment the chains that you wear. Pull out your favourite memories and get a silly smile on your face. *Pleasant memories, how they linger...*

Everybody tries to stack up memories against the depredations of time. That doesn't work so well. A memory is hardly different from a fantasy; it wears out over time. No memory can hold back the fall of night or the extinction of a star. Memories don't make a good wall because you can poke your mind right through them, right through to the other side. They don't accumulate. They don't stack up or add up to anything. Even a cornerstone memory can crumble away until very little is left but a face or a gesture or a cherry-picked landscape.

It's a scary thing to contemplate.

Whatever you have believed up till now is up for grabs. Whatever it is your tiny mind has grasped counts for nothing here, in the penumbra of the headstone, where the hard wind blows. Those wilted flowers you noted before, that mossy text, that seeding grass, the concrete angel, the fragrance of hospitals that never quite goes away: these are the real things. This is what you have come for, not some carrion comfort. Look around you. What you see is a graveyard of beliefs, a galaxy of headstones.

Forget the damned. The heads of believers tumble into the same buckets.

29

Here is a fragment from the bone of a bird a child found who strayed a little from the picnic. A slender wedge of skull. It lies easily in the palm of her hand, unmoving. It doesn't make any fuss. It is still flying through the earth, hardly touching the sides of matter. For this tachyon bird, the earth might as well be empty space. It has long since left its cement wings behind. It sings of all things bright and beautiful, and leaves no trace of its passing.

The child takes the wedge of skull and gravely places it before the headstone. I am touched. This child has just understood something it might take a lifetime to learn.

The tachyon bird flies on regardless, even through collapsing suns and dense neutron stars. The skull rests content before the headstone. It has been well picked over, like a story in a classroom or a scene from a familiar play. A little skull like that belongs up on a windowsill with the rest of the bric-a-brac. The stories are now all packed away or lie discarded in dusty corners. Even the story about the bird's skull, and how a little kid found it at a picnic, has been forgotten. Soon nobody will know how it got up there. All the little bits that might add up to something have been shoved into the closet, or thrown away. Or have ended up in a garage sale.

That's as it has to be. The child forgets her moment by the headstone.

But somebody risked going to heaven and incurring the wrath of gods to secure that story, and others, and to bring them back to earth. Somebody put their neck on the line for that bird's skull. In one case it was a plucky spider who did that, who spun a web all the way to the top of the headstone. There he had to do a deal with the gods for a basket of stories that he promised to take to the picnic.

Instead, he opened the basket, took out all the stories and wove them into his web. For the spider, the web is a story made up of strands of sound. It must hold that balance between fragility and strength. It must span the most unlikely spaces on the promise of a syllable.

The web clings to the side of the world where it is carefully attached. It is linked by its syllables to an empty centre. When you were a child you practiced sleeping in the sky, in the empty centre. You sang yourself to sleep intoning those syllables which resonated like a tuning fork. There was nowhere else to lie. The ground was too hard and the beds were too full. There is always a singularity at the centre of the spider's web. It is a good dream catcher. Incy-wincy spider knows all about catching dreams, spinning them in a silk coffin, saving them up for a rainy day. Stories to tell children. *Along came a spider and sat down beside her...*

You, sleeping peacefully in the still centre of the sky, knew nothing of the world, or the invisible bird, or the silver yarn that threads the suns into a bracelet for the headstone.

30

The headstone is of very few words, remember, a pious phrase or two – all the rest is made-up. *Less is more*, that's the motto. Just a handful of leaves on a grave, no more. Some sentiments sprinkled about sparingly; a little salt on the wound. Some scoring in the stone. A cement bird with tachyon wings that can fly right through the headstone without touching a single atom. It comes from a universe of virtual creatures, fields of zero mass grazed by neutrino dreams. *That's all you know and all you need to know.*

All those stories you liked to tell yourself have gone home to sleep it off. The right words get harder to find the further you move along the orbit of the headstone. In the outer regions of the headstone, there are hardly any words at all; a single syllable will stretch right around the universe.

Now, when you must have heard a thousand stories, lived a thousand stories, you can't even think of one. How ridiculous. *A Thousand and One Nights* and they are all a blur. That's not a good look. *There was a poor man who had two daughters, a king who had two sons... there was a fisherman who married a seal... there was a spider who went to heaven... there was an island that sank under a weight of gold... there was a king who followed a white antelope... a kiss blown into the wind will heal a leper.*

They are all there on the tip of your tongue, but that is not much use. All the tip of your tongue can do is quiver. You don't want to be caught in the middle of nowhere without some kind of backup; it helps to know what to say. It helps to have the book of rules at hand. It would look suspicious to leave you naked and without a name. That doesn't sound too promising. When time resumes its normal course, everything will be all right, surely. Good old business as usual; there's a lot to be said for it.

With money in the pocket and love in the heart, you can't go wrong, you figure. What else is there?

31

With the world in spin, you hardly dare to look, in case you get vertigo. With everything shifting so fast in relation to everything else, there is nowhere to just be. It's not just language that is never at rest, it's everything. Even death might not provide the closure you were looking for.

When you locate me in your fish-eye, the headstone ceases to somersault through the days. It stabilizes near the *Keep Off The Grass* sign where people like to picnic. Its pedigree is solid rock; it lays claim to a piece of earth. It insists that memory occupy a physical space; that there be place to stand, a place to put flowers. A place to face whatever has to be faced.

Your eyes are fixed on the headstone. It's a referent, like a compass point. It stands out against the background noise. Yes, I am here, but I can stay with you for only so long, and that long is almost done. Soon I will no longer be the headstone and you will no longer be you. Then it'll be *so long, it's been good to know you.*

Becoming aware of this, you are afraid to look away in case everything disappears. Nothing left but the leftovers – a piece of flattened grass where the kids played hopscotch. If only you'd paid attention at the time, you might have been able to snare one of those moments hurtling past and got a grip on yourself.

The world is waiting out there, beyond the blindfold. That's not a promise, it's a start. There's a lot of coming and going.

The headstone has an unrushed simplicity about it, the way it is shaped, the way it sits in the earth, inviting your devotion. No bustle no hustle. No traffic jams. No parking tickets.

At the right moment it all comes out to play. The great hullabaloo.

Everything you see around you, everything you once called your own, has arisen from that laughter and pain and is buried in the brow of the headstone, where I keep it safe. There is a landscape which comes up out of the water shedding its sparkles, pulled to the surface by a determined hand. It is the cosmos, spreadeagled on love. It is freshly borne out of the sighs and whispers of shadow and light. It is a land which exists in its fragrances. It has no bone to pick with memory. It doesn't carry any ancestors on its back like a pile of heavy sticks. The fire that sparks from the rubbing of the sky and earth discharges into you. *Slam, slam!* It all begins with that first tingle. The flash across the electric skin. From that moment you are a goner. Beyond salvation.

set me up
and knock me over like a feather.

32

A moment will come of such enchantment it will take your breath away. For good. That is as it should be. If anything is going to steal the breath from your ribcage it should be rapture.

After all, everything is making whoopee.

You can get up now. Arise! You can dance on the headstone. You can wave your limbs in the air. You can fart in the wind. You can make love to a sugar spoon. All is possible in the most impossible of words. *And the little dog laughed to see such craft and the dish ran away with the spoon!*

The best part of it is, there's no need to breathe anymore. You have paid the ferryman in true coin. Yours is now the breath of stars. Your sorrows have washed away in the waters of forgetfulness. Your tears dry on your cheeks. Your laughter still makes the circuit of your mouth. Your hands come together and fall part. You fall by the headstone, by the wayside. You smell the grass.

Forever is the pretence. If the tears don't dry, let them fall. It's over to them now to take care of their sorrows. Let each tear crawl away into the earth with its little burden, its secret. Like glaucous insects, tears will crawl away into the little cracks and crannies of memory. Everything that grows around here is watered by grief, that's how your garden grows.

You don't ask the earth to swallow you up. You just lie down on the grass to have a little snooze and the ground opens up beneath your dreams and you fall between the cracks, right slap into the headstone. You are less than happy to see me. In me, dreams come to an end. The words run out of fizz.

You have come from a long way away, but it doesn't feel like that. It feels like you have just come down in the last shower of rain, or tears. You give over your innocence in return for gladness. You have your immunity now, that makes the difference. Let memory go off in search of breath. You can stay behind.

You can make the moment with the flowers possible.

33

You'll never make it to your destination. Destinations don't mean much around here; objectives are a dime a dozen. You can't turn around without running into somebody's game plan. Everybody has another sure-fire shortcut but destinations themselves are on the move. The goalposts are always shifting. When the earth opens and swallows you up without a nod or a wink, you know the trail has petered out.

All kinds of screwy logic come into play. Superstitious thinking breaks out like a rash. Destinations create distances and distances create appetite, and appetite in turn stretches the world into impossible places. Prayers may wither on the vine without notice, or blossom unseen in the lotus heart. This isn't a railway station, or a pit stop. I'm not selling tickets. We headstones are not stops along a highway, with people and cafes and car parks, airports and corridors and hurrying and scurrying. That's all memory. That was Main Street back in the day, with cars, concerts and carnivals. It's all a one-way street now, a city of dead ends. A city of people walking around looking for a place to arrive, and there's a god on every street corner. Everybody has to watch out for that. Let the believer beware.

People may arrive but find it harder to leave. All destinations are buried in the headstone; here, there and everywhere. Everything comes to a stop. You mill about with the others, not knowing what to say. There are plenty of emergency sandwiches, and the picnic basket is full of flowers. Polite talk runs its course. The kids start playing hopscotch. Soldiers start moving in with sandbags. You were starting to wonder if you were getting anywhere or if the world was just moving around you. That's quite fitting. You never arrived and you never left, imagine that! You have always been here, just as the figure by your side has never strayed from the path. You never needed all those destinations in the first place. At the gate, the traffic sign announces, *Slow Down, You Are Already Here.*

34

Distances don't measure well. Like destinations, they tend to get lost in translation. How far can a mouse run up the clock? No further than from midnight to dawn. That fabled piece of string is as long as it is; when it runs out of long, then it isn't. Where there is no time, there is no distance.

Grief might account for distances. The time it takes for an ordinary, everyday tear to travel down your cheek is the time it takes to go there and back again. How far can tears burrow into the earth? All the way to the bones. The same bones that have been washed with tears and then put away to rot. Each tear carries a world with it, on its back. Its distances are purely emotional. It's not a very long road from one sorrow, one regret, one grief, to the next. These things come in bundles. Hot tears may crawl away but they won't get far. They're on a leash.

What is the distance between one side of the headstone and the other? No distance at all as the crow flies. Can you measure it with your hands, or in heartbeats? Impossible to tell.

I'm in the gap between the here and there and the back again. That gap into which they throw their lives, one hour after the other like good money after bad. People look everywhere. They'll sometimes meet themselves coming the other way. Because this is a paradox, they pretend they haven't seen themselves. Once they get here they settle down, throw a blanket over the grass and unpack the picnic basket. Out come all the goodies. Distances are forgotten, destinations are relegated to mythology. Journeys are folded up a like a pack of cards. You have a whole world to play in yet never have to move a step. Nothing going anywhere, just marking time, jogging on the spot.

There are no distances within the headstone. I admit to no latitude and longitude. Triangulate all you like, I'm not there. I'm not to be found with compass and set-square, rulers and theodolites.

Turn the headstone sideways and it vanishes from view.

Appearances are deceptive, and our language lets us down every time. There is always a distance from one end of a sentence to the other. Games get played. People put good money down on a word or three. But you can't trust a single syllable. Sometimes it seems like a long climb to get to the end of a sentence – only to find that it hasn't really ended.

Destination is a word it takes a long time to say, as there are plenty of syllables, lots of stops along the way, lots of picnics and barking dogs. Even destiny's a shorter trip; the end's already written. But the headstone has no ends either. No sides, no ends. Rotate it through space and it might disappear, taking space with it.

Given all this, joy is never far away. In joy, all distances collapse and become one another. Joy has no destination, and it always comes as a surprise. Joy haunts the evening cypress with a song.

You put your best foot forward and the world just slides underneath you. Everybody laughs.

Now you know about distances.

Now you can leave them behind.

35

The headstone is a four-dimensional object in a three-dimensional world, that's the bugger of it. We can only see the part of it that three dimensions allow; the rest is hidden around the corner of time and space. That needn't be too disconcerting, even if it is.

It might come as a relief to know that these three dimensions are not all there is. Height, width and depth can't tell the whole story of the headstone. Even adding time as an extra dimension doesn't help much. There are more dimensions rolled up and hidden away in the tiniest of places. You can hammer on the walls but they won't come out to play.

Why don't you sit a bit closer, snuggle up a little. If there are no distances, why be so stand-offish? Mistaken shyness can be costly. We don't stand on ceremony around here. People laugh or cry under the sun, you can do the same. Kids draw squares on the ground and jump about. No matter how much this space fills up, it never gets overcrowded. There's always room for one more, or two. There's no competition for distances here; the emptiness is endless. The blood and clay are so mixed there's no telling one from the other.

It's a very big back lawn. If you snuggle up close no one will say anything. Confessions of love are not a crime. Love goes with the turf. My turf. There's no excuse for all this otherwise. Love is not a feeling, it is a mode of apprehension, a way of seeing. Love transforms what it sees. Words fade into space as the stars rise up through the headstone.

Snuggle up close enough and the concrete angel will lean its head against your shoulder. You may whisper your secrets into its ear, if that's what you want, until you are all whispered out. Broken tongues have spoken. That's the key to understanding the headstone. I have no secrets. No esoteric knowledge of any kind. Just the simple observation: *Here lies....*

I don't bite, you know. You'll get used to it, once you get over the vertigo. You can take all the time you need to appreciate that you are safe, that nobody is watching. The children are playing hopscotch in the air and the adults are drinking beer under the ground. The lovers are lying in the grass. Nobody is taking any notice of you or me, or the hush that comes between us.

And if you have any doubts, remember the moment when your tears declared their independence and crawled off to find their own lives. Like little insects with shiny backs, you will remember that. All the nooks and crannies. Those tears are now dissolved in the alchemy of the headstone. You can rest your head here, and feel the softness of the wind.

36

The world rises up against itself. Gods do battle on darkling plains. Ignorant armies clash by night. Flowing foxfire lights the battleground. Unquiet spirits gather around. An ancient darkness breaks over earth and heaven. The prophets point from one to the other. The headstone points both ways, to life-in-death and death-in-life. Words go their own merry way unless they are reminded of their duties to truth, honour and justice. I try to take care of that side of things. I pour a libation for funeral rights. I spin the wheel of invocation. I invite all-comers to share the picnic. No soul left behind.

I am always happy to see a spirit on the rise.

They say god, whichever you name, divided his genderless self from himself in order to create sentient beings. She submitted herself to the paradox of creation. Now she pays the price. The world rises up against itself in a fury of forgetfulness. That forgetfulness is god's as much as it is man's. *In the beginning was the word,* and the word was the first act of remembrance.

The words on the headstone are always quite simple. *Herein lies a good man. Here lies a beloved mother. You will be remembered.*

Lest we forget.

One day somebody might pass by, somebody like you, maybe carrying a picnic basket, and they will stop and say, 'Look here is an unremembered grave, let's pause here for a moment and remember it, let's say a quick prayer for this forgotten soul. And they will say a quick prayer and for a moment you will remember, and a spark will catch in the headstone. Your memories will find redress in the neural pathways of the sky beyond the battle of the gods, beyond the fields of necessary flowers. The figure by your side will remind you that you already know this place. You played here as a child. You caught someone's thought and spun it in your fingers until it turned gold.

Nothing is lost. It becomes the stuff of new suns, new gods, skies as fresh as daisies. And there you are, between the memory and the prayer, the headstone and the grave – the hop, the skip and the jump.

Right with me now and ever more.

37

You thought there would be something more than this, didn't you? You are having last minute doubts even though it's too late for that. The flower seller has packed away her things. Here comes memory with its pooper-scooper. We've been through all that, you and I. We have a history. It's not the same as calling it quits.

These fragments, these bits and pieces we have turned over in our hands are not enough for you. You feel so distant from them, like an archaeologist holding some shards of pottery from an unknown culture. You have no way of fitting them together let alone decoding them. On the other hand you know them well: the shard of bird's skull on the window sill; the skipping rope hanging from a clothes-peg; the cockroach that climbed out of the drain.

They all pass through your fingers like sand, like breadcrumbs, like leftovers, and the emptiness is still there. It is the emptiness of unloved rooms. Dry leaves blowing down the valley. Moonlight on river ice. You insist that all this must add up to something. That the equation puts weight back into the world. You want it all spelled out word by word, line by line, verse by verse. You are chasing filamentary strings of meaning. Words in clusters, super clusters, clusters of super clusters. You want to look out over another page of creation as if you were god. Another and another, page after page. Be careful what you wish for, they say.

There has to be a key or code, you reason. Some Rosetta Stone of consciousness that will enable you to translate all this into meaningful sequences. Disparate, apparently random things, conjoining in an apparently random moment, must have some purpose, some pattern. Everything has a purpose, even the headstone. All you lack is the code, the key to the code. Something to unlock the fragrance. Until you have that you have nothing but a jumble of letters on a headstone, each letter pointing in a different direction, towards different worlds. Ants scurrying out; ants scurrying in.

That doesn't take you very far.

It all adds up to zero; that's what you fear. When the equation is all balanced out there is and will be nothing left, not even the scraps that fall from the table. All the bits and bytes, humps and lumps all add up to one great big fat nothing. That's what the laws of physics tell us: that the energy balance of the whole mighty universe adds up to nothing. A finely balanced zero. A mossy vase and a passing parade of flowers.

Here are cities, blinded by feathers and rain, living on borrowed energy. The moths have returned to their nocturnal world. We won't see their like again on earth. Someone has taken the lid off the sky. It's wide open now. Voiceless, the mourners pass through us. They stroll through drifts of scarlet poppies. All their songs now rest in peace.

Only the headstone is left over, and that's a bit of a laugh as far as I'm concerned. The headstone, too, is living on borrowed energy. You've come a long way to get to this place which doesn't even turn out to be a destination in any proper sense. Now the long way has gone too, swallowed up by the even handed terms of the equation. It's all borrowed energy, as far as you can see. Then it's payback time. End of story. End of not-story.

It's not enough to stand before it with your face in your hands. You want to touch me. You want to know what happens to a mystery when you hug it. You want to reach out and grasp the letters on the headstone, to reach right through them to the other side.

The other side of the zero.

38

Now is the time to do a final stocktake, collect all these rag-tag remnants and give them all a last makeover. Open up the rooms and give them an airing, knock out a few walls. Let the wind blow low, let the wind blow high; there's always a fresh spring wind blowing somewhere. Sounds of laughter are close to home. There's rapture in the wheat fields when the gale gets up. To their scattered bodies, the people go. Home from over the hill through clouds of asphodels.

Take a bit of spit-and-polish to your options, the ones

gathering dust, the ones lived and hardly lived. A bit of elbow grease is all that's needed. *Rub-a-dub-bub.* Some of these virtual lives, born from multiple probabilities, shine up like mother-of-pearl, all polished and lucent. Some don't. Some get left behind after the picnic, scraps for the sparrows and the ants. Now that it's time to go home, old fears take familiar forms. Baba Yaga waits at the corner of the street gnashing her iron teeth, her eyes aglow with desire.

There's no longer any home, not as you imagine it. Home is where the headstone lies – but there is something else, something nobody counted on. It's the hole in the zero. I'm not the first to notice it: the loophole, the sinkhole, the bolthole, and backhole. It's well referenced; you can look it up. It survived all the wars through the pages of a book. You may fall through it, tumble through it. A cockroach crawled through it. It doesn't change. It is in itself the ground zero of change.

Pull up a time and place. Set a space. Paint it if you like; there's a palette of colours available. Sit down and chew the fat with everybody. It's no good dancing all over the place, whizzing about like a fly in a bottle or a kite on a string. There'll always be a hole in the zero, which is buried deep in the headstone and so can never be lost. It's in there with all our histories. If you forget the song, you can always make up the words – there are plenty of words lying around unattended. What there won't always be is this particular moment, the one in which you apprehend these things. The fulcrum. The moment at which all the forces leveraging off one another hit the jackpot.

This is a singular one-off instant never to be repeated. It is a unique constellation that exists only in the moment that it is revealed. This flash here, before the headstone.

You feel like a child who hasn't yet learned to read. You stand before a mystery with your head bowed. You know nothing about crossing a 't' or dotting an 'i'. Mobius-strip sentences twist in the middle and join at the ends. You stand before the impossible, the never-ending word, the long chant.

Everything looks different now. The headstone looms up massive and dense. You want to turn away but there is no away, turn as you might. You comfort yourself with the thought that once you have learned to read, a world of secrets will be revealed to you. So many secrets! You look forward to breaking the code and learning the sequence, the magic sequence. The magic syllables which, when uttered throw open every doorway and abolish horizons in favour of bliss.

And yet, the most profound of all secrets is being revealed to you every time you look out at the world – if you could only see what you are seeing.

If you can know, can have your being, can be here now, in every astonishment, long after my words have stopped – and the headstone has fallen silent...

... then we'll know you've got somewhere at long last.